Careful 小心 Enough?

Dillon Forbes

JOURNEYFORTH
Greenville, South Carolina

Library of Congress Cataloging-in-Publication Data

Forbes, Dillon.
  Careful enough? / Dillon Forbes.
    p. cm.
  Summary: Seventeen-year-old Daniel's plan to become a missionary
is put on the fast-track when his parents take him to China, but his hope
to bring at least one person to the Lord is complicated by the need to
hide their mission from communist sympathizers.
  ISBN 978-1-59166-835-0 (perfect bound pbk. : alk. paper)
  [1. Missionaries—Fiction. 2. Christian life—Fiction. 3. Communism—
Fiction. 4. Family life—China—Fiction. 5. China—Fiction.] I. Title.
  PZ7.F7486Car 2008
  [Fic]—dc22

                                                                    2007048404

Cover photos: Craig Oesterling (men); iStockphoto.com © Wolfgang
    Kaiser (wall)
Interior photo: © CoolCLIPS.com. 2008

Design by Nick Ng
Page layout by Kelley Moore

© 2008 by BJU Press
Greenville, SC 29614
JourneyForth Books is a division of BJU Press

Printed in the United States of America

ISBN 978-1-59166-835-0

15 14 13 12 11 10 9 8 7 6 5 4 3 2 1

To the people
who helped me write this book,
who make it more fact than fiction.

CONTENTS

ONE

Sweeping noises startled me awake. 5:47 in the morning and someone was already cleaning the courtyard below. Couldn't they wait?

But never mind that. It was Sunday. I was going to my first house church service in Communist China. Would we get raided? How should I act? Who would be there?

A day and a half earlier my family had landed in Huajiang*, a Chinese city of nine million people. It was my decision really. In March of my junior year in high school my math teacher dad and receptionist mom had felt God leading them to be missionaries to China. Secret missionaries. Their visa applications read "Brett Wheeler—math teacher" and "Emily Wheeler—housewife." Which was true. Dad would be teaching and Mom would be keeping house. But their real reason for the career change was to bring the gospel to China. They wanted to help our friends Chuck and Susan Harvey start a house church.

* fictional city

Mom and Dad said they could move to China after I finished my senior year of homeschool and left for Bible college. But sooner would be better. They left it up to me. If I was willing, we could go as a family in five months.

No pressure, Daniel. You don't mind leaving your friends and youth group and everything you've ever known to be a secret missionary in a dangerous place, do you? Or we could wait a year. We could put off God's will for our lives and make the Harveys wait when they desperately need help.

They didn't say it like that. They just told me the decision was up to me. So after five months of packing and waiting for visas, I was in China.

I parted the curtains and gazed down on the courtyard six floors below. Some white-haired Chinese people in dark baggy pants were practicing tai chi six floors below. These people were our new neighbors. We lived in a six-story building with seven stairwells. Each stairwell had two apartments on each floor. How many neighbors did that make? Then there were the other nine buildings in our complex.

I gave up on the math. Was I supposed to witness to my new neighbors or keep quiet and play it safe?

Somehow safety and China didn't go together. I thought back five months to when the tsunami of news first struck.

We had been eating chocolate cake left over from the missionary conference where our friends Chuck and Susan had presented their ministry in China. Mom and Dad dropped the bombshell. If I was willing, we could be in China in five months.

I had asked if it was safe to be a missionary in China. Dad said that we weren't going to say that word in our home anymore. The M-word—*missionary.*

He said that in China we would only use words like *Christian* and *church* very carefully with people we felt we could trust. But we could never use the M-word. He said it was legal to be a Christian in China, but a missionary—that was different. If anyone in China asked why we had come, we could answer that Dad was a teacher. We could say that our family had come to China to experience another culture and to see China's scenery.

"Is it safe to witness in China?" I had asked. "Is it legal?"

Dad had answered that it was never right to lie, but we would not say more than we needed to about certain things. We would try to stay within the law as much as possible, but in the end we just had to place ourselves in God's hands and trust Him.

We wouldn't pass out tracts, but would find other ways to witness—creative ways. Chuck had said that there are lots of things they can't do to share the gospel, but they focus on what they can do. We would do that too.

My brain had been full of question marks that night, but what can you say when your parents' faces are glowing with anticipation? It was up to me. We could go as a family now, or my parents would go without me in a year.

Earlier in the year, after a different missionary spoke, I told the Lord I'd be a missionary if that's what He wanted. I told Him I'd go anywhere anytime. I thought I meant it at the time. But I had thought *anywhere* would be some safe mission field where they spoke an easy language like Spanish. And *anytime* surely meant anytime after four years of Bible college and a few years of deputation. Now the Lord seemed to be saying, "China. Now."

Finally I gave in. "OK, Lord," I prayed. "I'll go to China. I'll eat weird things and try to learn Chinese and do what I can to help. But I need to know that you can use me. I want to sit down with one person, explain salvation to him, and listen to him say the sinner's prayer. If You do that, I'll know that you want me in missions."

I felt I had been very reasonable with God, even generous . . . until the day after The Big Decision when I told Melody about it while I drove us to symphony practice.

Melody Matthews and I had a strange and wonderful relationship. You couldn't call it dating because the two of us dating would just be too weird. Together we practiced my cello and her violin. And we polished our arguing skills to near perfection without either of us getting mad. I figure a really fine argument beats basketball any day.

When I told Melody, she tossed her head, swinging strawberry blond hair behind her shoulders. "I think your parents are asking a lot to expect you to leave all your friends and go to a country where being a Christian is illegal."

"Actually, it's not illegal to be a Christian. It's illegal to go to an unregistered church. And it's illegal for a foreigner to try to convert Chinese. But anyone can be a Christian."

"So what are you going to do in China?"

"I guess we'll try to convert Chinese and start an unregistered church, but we'll do whatever we can to make it as legal as possible."

"Daniel, you are so weird. Can't you do anything normal? If you're going to be a missionary, can't you go to some normal mission field where missions is legal?"

I had told her I'd be careful and follow Chuck's guidelines for how and when to share the gospel. I told her that I'd be careful not to do anything stupid, but I wanted more than safety. I wanted God to use me. I wanted God to help me lead one soul to Christ all by myself. If the Lord would help me to do that, I would become a missionary.

Melody had asked if that wasn't bargaining with God. If God is God, she had said, wasn't He supposed to set the conditions?

"Hey, Gideon put a fleece out to make sure what God wanted him to do. Leading a person to the Lord is my fleece."

"I hope you can win someone to the Lord, Daniel, and I'll pray for you. But you'll have to admit that the whole idea is pretty bizarre."

Bizarre. Weird. Strange. Extreme. Odd. If she had given me a thesaurus, I would have come up with some more. But this bizarre idea had become God's plan for my life. And now, five months later, Dad was a math teacher who taught English in China. I was actually living in China and getting ready to go to my first house church service.

I grabbed my Bible and lay back on my bed. "Lord make me brave," I prayed. "I know it will take a while to get adjusted to my new life. But once things settle down, could you give me a job to do? I know my parents are the missionar—you know, Lord. The M-word. But I want to do something too."

After breakfast my parents and I trekked down five flights of stairs. If a building only had six stories in China, it didn't have to have an elevator. I'd be getting a lot of exercise.

Chuck had introduced us to the bus system the day before when we visited them. We knew how to find our way to his house where the church group met. He also gave us a card with his address and our own. If we ever got lost, we could call a taxi or pedicab. Now we'd find out how well we understood his instructions.

We stood at the number 12 bus stop. We three average, brown-haired Americans looked far less average among the crowd of short, black-haired people who pushed past us. Masses of cars, buses, scooters, and bikes filled the eight lanes of traffic in front of us. A three-wheeled bicycle called a pedicab passed close to our feet. The Chinese driver leaned forward on the pedals, trying to gain momentum to pull his two passengers. Then I spotted a shiny, new, motorized three-wheeled car.

I pointed to it. "I want to ride one of those sometime."

Mom smiled. "Well, Daniel, I imagine you will get to ride in many of those. And the bicycle thingies, and buses, and trains. You name it." She stepped off the curb to read the number on an approaching bus.

An electric scooter shot past soundlessly, nearly knocking Mom off her feet.

"You OK, Mom?"

She grabbed Dad's arm and stepped back onto the curb. "Yes, dear. Susan said China can be an adventure or a nightmare. It's all in how you look at it. I fully intend to make it an adventure."

The number 12 bus pulled up then and the three of us squeezed in the door. Dad and I grabbed a pole. Mom grabbed Dad. The bus lurched forward. I braced my feet and tried not to lean against the lady in front of me. To get a better grip I set my shopping bag on the floor, pulling it to one side so no one could see the three Bibles inside. What would these people think if they knew we were on our way to an illegal house church?

At each stop people got on and off. I was pushed farther toward the front of the bus. Mom and Dad were pushed toward the back. Before long I only got occasional glimpses of Dad's receding hairline and Mom's curly brown hair. Would we lose each other? I had all I could do to stay balanced, holding onto a pole, wedged into a knot of people. I hoped my deodorant was working.

I edged toward the window to see the Chinese streets and watch for our destination. Over heads and between arms that gripped poles I studied the streets of Huajiang. Tall concrete buildings with giant Chinese signs flew past. McDonald's. Pizza Hut. These were reassuring, but I didn't come all the way to China to eat at McDonald's. Little shops crammed themselves between large buildings. People were everywhere. Dressed up ladies and students in uniforms waited for buses. Old people pedaled bicycles beside young people talking on cell phones. Huajiang made Seattle's streets look empty.

Crowded. Noisy. Strange. My new home. Adventure or nightmare—only a fine line separated the two. Would I ever find my way around this city of nine million? What was I doing here?

Twenty minutes into our ride I spotted it. A Subway and a Pizza Hut by a statue of a dragon. Our stop. I couldn't see Mom and Dad, but I shoved toward the side door of the bus. No time to be polite.

Dad's face appeared over the top of a girl's head. *Is this it?* he mouthed.

I nodded.

The bus rolled to a stop. We wiggled out while other passengers wiggled in. Chuck, with his red hair, stood head and shoulders above the Chinese waiting at the bus stop.

Dad dabbed at the sweat trickling from his forehead. "We made it! I was afraid we wouldn't. We got separated on the bus, and I wondered if we'd end up spread all over Huajiang."

Chuck laughed. "I forgot to tell you. If you want to stay together on a bus, you've all got to lean the same direction when people start pushing. You'll get the hang of it."

We strolled towards the Harveys' apartment building. I glanced up at all the tall buildings and noticed how much the concrete buildings with their tiled sides looked alike. I was glad Chuck had met us at the bus stop.

I leaned over to Chuck and whispered. "I can't believe we're going to a house church."

"Yeah, well, we usually just say our group is getting together. The C-word is good, but in China *group* is a safer word. And we haven't organized into a real C yet." He waved to a couple of girls. "There's Daisy. She always wears that daisy barrette in her hair, so it's easy to remember her. I wonder who's with her."

Two girls smiled and sauntered over to us. "Hi, Chuck. This is Fiona, my friend. She come to study Bible. Is it OK?"

I searched the courtyard. She said *Bible* right out loud. Did the man reading the newspaper hear her?

Chuck stepped closer and lowered his voice. "Hi, Fiona. It's nice to meet you. How do you know Daisy?"

Daisy answered. "Fiona is my classmate. I tell her I learn Bible from you, and she want to learn Bible too. I know I should ask you before, but Fiona ask me questions I cannot answer. Is it OK?"

Chuck smiled. "Let's go upstairs, shall we?"

We climbed four flights of stairs. Mom and Dad had to rest their legs after three.

Once inside we took off our shoes. Susan offered us slippers, but they were intended for smaller Chinese feet. I skipped the slippers, enjoying the cool tiles on my sock feet. Susan offered us each a cup of tea and introduced us to Max and Jason who were already there. We nodded to each and found seats around the Harveys' comfortable living room. I wondered if the average Chinese home was as clean and nice as this one.

Daisy set her tea on the coffee table. "I tell Fiona Ten Commandments. One commandment is we must not kill. Is it right? Fiona want to know is it wrong to kill cockroach?"

Was she joking? No. Maybe they believed in reincarnation here. Chuck explained the difference between murder, which the commandment meant, and other killing like accidental death or killing animals.

Several others knocked at the door, and Susan let them in. Soon eleven Chinese and five Americans circled the living room. I couldn't tell what age they were, but no one was much younger than I was, and no one looked older than my parents.

We chatted about the weather and the exams some of them were taking. Then Chuck asked us to open our Bibles to Acts 8.

Leaning back in his armchair with his legs crossed, he discussed the Ethiopian who wanted to know about Jesus. As he told about Philip approaching the chariot, the doorbell rang, and Susan let a youngish man in.

Chuck explained what an Ethiopian was. A guy named Max broke in. During introductions Chuck had told us that Max, an engineer, had been saved just over a year. "This week I read the book of the Bible called Song of Solomon." He opened his Bible. "It says, 'Look not upon me, because I am black, because the sun hath looked upon me.' Is it bad to have dark skin?"

I decided if Max had only been saved a year and he was trying to understand the Song of Solomon, he was doing pretty well. Still, it wasn't the kind of question I expected to be answering in China.

Chuck was telling about the Ethiopian being baptized by the time Sunny got there. She slipped out of her shoes and joined the circle with no apologies.

So this was what a house church was like. Or a potential house church. The group hadn't organized into a church yet. No singing. No offering. No kids. Just a bunch of people sitting around the Harveys' living room talking about the Bible. People asked questions as they came up. I wondered if all house churches were like this one.

Chuck talked quite a bit about baptism. He was planning a baptism in the near future and hoped some of the group would be ready to be baptized. After the baptism we would organize into a church. The Bible study ended. Our family shifted around to talk to various people. I switched chairs to talk to Jason, who looked about my age.

Jason chatted about our trip and what I thought of Huajiang. We discovered Jason was only a year older than I was, though my average American body dwarfed his. Jason rode the bus from his dormitory an hour one way to come to the Bible studies. Sunday morning he left in time to catch the 11:45 train to his home in the country. Monday morning he took an early train back to the university in time for class.

"Chuck tell me you are Christian many years. I think you must know much about Bible."

I shrugged. "Well, yeah, I guess so. I mean, I got saved when I was six. I've been going to church all of my life, and we study the Bible at home. I should have learned something in all of that time."

"Maybe you will teach me Bible? Maybe we will be friends? I think you are good person to teach me Bible."

Chuck crept up behind us. "Jason got saved a few weeks ago. I thought you might like to disciple him, but I haven't had a chance to talk to you about it yet."

I *had* asked God for a job, but I hadn't expected this big of a job on my second full day in China. I didn't even know Chinese yet. But then Chuck and Susan didn't know Chinese when they first came to China either. They taught English Bible studies while they learned Chinese. Now that Dad and Mom could help with the English studies, Chuck and Susan would be able to do more in Chinese.

I had learned about ten words of Chinese vocabulary from a CD I had checked out of the Seattle library. I knew how to take the number 12 bus from our house to Harveys'. And Chuck thought I was ready to disciple a Chinese believer. At least I could do it in English.

This was the fastest answer to prayer I had ever seen. Maybe next time I would pray a little slower. Living in China was going to be one wild ride.

TWO

In fifth grade I had two exceptionally smart friends. We formed our own secret agent club and actually formulated a code which we were sure no one could crack. We used the code to send very important, top secret messages to each other. One highly sensitive document roughly translated said, "Sierra Hanson has lips like a camel and a neck like a giraffe."

I felt like a fifth grader all over again. Chuck had warned us that our e-mails and phone calls could be monitored. After Sunday lunch with the Harveys they offered to let us use their computer to e-mail friends. We might not have internet access in our home for weeks.

I had just been to my first meeting of a house church. I couldn't wait to tell Melody all about it, but I knew I couldn't use words like *church* or *Christian* or *God*. What could I say?

Mom e-mailed Aunt Jenny in Seattle while I tried to figure out what to say to Melody. Aunt Jenny wanted to know everything about our ministry in China. She and Uncle Mike had asked me to live with them next summer while I got ready to go to Bible college.

When Mom finished I wrote Melody.

Dear Melody,

Today I got to meet the group. Our friends ask weird and unpredictable questions like you do. Like—if we aren't supposed to kill, can we kill cockroaches? In the first half of the book we love there's a poetry section about the king and his wife. It's not a part I read very much. It talks about having dark skin. One person wondered if that was bad. They seem to like light skin here. In fact, some people have umbrella holders on the handlebars of their bicycles. They stick open umbrellas in the holders to protect them from the sun. Funny how Americans are always trying to get their skin darker and Chinese do the opposite.

I have a new Chinese friend named Jason. He wants to study with me. I will help him with his English, and I'm sure he'll help me with my almost nonexistent Chinese. I also plan to talk to him about things that are more important to me. He is like a new brother to me. So when you think about how I need help, remember this.

It's almost time for you to leave for college. I hope you get a lot out of your studies. I also hope you get a very patient roommate. She will have to be to put up with you. (Ha, ha.)

Daniel

I re-read my letter hoping Melody would understand how to pray for me. She was smarter than I liked to admit. She'd figure it out.

Our family spent most of our first week in China learning to live.

Chuck taught us our first Chinese lesson. We learned various greetings and replies and how to count to ten in Chinese.

Susan walked us to the market where we could buy fresh vegetables and fruit from various stalls. We visited a supermarket. Susan showed us how to tell baking powder from cornstarch in packages which were labeled only in Chinese.

Mom gave me a hundred yuan, which is worth a little more than ten US dollars, and let me buy snacks for our family. I roamed through stores and market stalls in our area and came home with quite a selection. My favorite were some chewy little sesame balls. The worst? Little round pastries with bitter black stuff inside. But I couldn't read the labels even when there were labels, and a lot of things were made locally and weren't prepackaged.

Buying breakfast was also my job. I could get bags of fresh soybean milk and steamed bread or meat dumplings from a little shop. Fruit stands sold ordinary fruit and little green fragrant melons or pomelos. Boxes of American cereal were way too expensive. We could have oatmeal or eggs when I didn't feel like trekking down five flights of stairs—which was every morning. But what was I doing in China if I wasn't going to embrace the experience?

Each morning I would say to myself, "What's it going to be—adventure or oatmeal?" And down I'd go.

It wasn't fancy, but our little apartment was clean, and the concrete walls were freshly painted. Mom and Dad bought the most basic wooden furniture with cushions, a small refrigerator, and a gas hot plate to cook on. Dad insisted Mom buy a regular American washing machine even though it was hugely expensive. Mom also bought a couple of Chinese scrolls to hang on the walls and a small rug for the tile floor in the living room. We were ready for visitors.

I called Jason on his cell phone and invited him to our house for lunch. After lunch we'd do our first Bible study. Chuck had suggested doing Bible studies with lunch so if anyone asked him why he came to our house he'd have a good excuse. Already we were learning the Christian strategies of being truthful and avoiding suspicion at the same time.

Jason brought rice and meat thingies wrapped in bamboo leaves. He called them *zongzi*. We offered him potato soup and peanut butter and banana sandwiches.

After lunch Jason and I found the most comfortable living room chairs. Mom brought us a plate of the chewy sesame seed balls.

"I think God send you to China to teach me Bible. I think I am very lucky to have American friend my same age teach Bible to me."

At least I didn't have to teach him in Chinese. I practiced counting to ten in Chinese and had Jason correct my tones.

Next Jason taught me the correct pronunciation for my Chinese name, Wu Dan. Chuck chose Wu for our surname because it started with a W like Wheeler. Daniel in the Bible was called Dan Yi Li. I chose the shortened form, Dan, to be more like Chinese one-syllable names.

Jason's Chinese name was Li Jing, but most of the Chinese in our group used their English names so they called him "Jason."

We studied the lesson in the book. It explained how a Christian could know for sure he was saved and how he could never lose his salvation. Then Jason asked his own questions.

"My grandfather was very good person. He help many people. For example, he buy extra rice and give to poor people. When my father was little boy, Grandfather drive him on bike to school every day very far. Grandfather never hear Bible." Jason's eyes locked onto mine. "Six years before now, Grandfather die. I want to know if Grandfather go to heaven when he die."

Stalling for time, I popped a sesame ball in my mouth. "Wow, Jason, I really wish I could say your grandfather is in heaven, but, you know, the Bible says that Jesus is the only way to heaven. Do you think there's any way he could have heard about God Who created the world? Did he know anything about Jesus dying on the cross?"

Jason shook his head.

"Sorry, Jason. I wish I had a different answer."

"The answer is no?"

"Yes. The answer is no. I'm sorry."

"I did not think so, but I want to ask you. I also want to know, can you teach me to pray?"

"Well, sure. You just talk to God. Like you would to me. Or you can think your prayer. God knows what you are thinking."

Jason folded his hands. "Chuck always hold hands like this when he pray. He always look down. Should I pray like Chuck?"

I shrugged. "Sure. That's a good way to pray. In Seattle in our church we always have the little kids fold their hands so they don't bother the person beside them. And we bow our heads because, well, it's kind of like bowing to a king, I guess."

"Children go to American church?"

"Of course."

"Many children go to church?"

"Sure. We have Sunday School. Kids of all ages come, and we have different classes. You know, we teach really simple stories for the little kids and harder ones for the older ones and teenagers. The adults even have their own class."

"America is very good place. In China children not allowed to go to church."

"Why not?"

Jason shrugged. "I do not know these things."

"Well, that's just wrong. The government has no right to tell parents they can't send their kids to church."

Jason hung his head. "China and America very different. So when pray you must hold hands together, bow head to God. Is this all?"

"Well, you can do that if you want. I always close my eyes so I can think about what I'm praying. Well, not always. When I was a kid I started praying while I was riding a bike. I closed my eyes and ran into a truck."

Jason covered his mouth. I noticed that Chinese cover their mouths when they laugh like an American covers his sneeze. "I think you must not do that, Daniel."

"I know that now. But you know what kids are like."

Jason's face turned serious. "I must ask one more question. I ask Jesus to forgive sins. Bible say Jesus do this. Chuck say every Christian should be baptized. Chuck say I must ask parents before I be baptized. My parents do not know I am Christian. They say Christians are very weak. My neighbor become Christian. Parents say 'What is wrong with Li Huo she become Christian? Why she need to learn Bible? Can she not be strong without religion?'"

"But Christians aren't weak for trusting God. No one is strong enough to handle all of life's problems by themselves. Everyone needs God."

"Chinese do not think this way. Chinese think self must be strong. Parents say must obey government, not talk bad about things government do. Parents say must work hard, must remember there is no gods."

"Oh, they want you to be an atheist. An atheist believes that there is no God."

He nodded.

I tried to picture a revival service for atheists. Christians tried to convert you so that you would be saved. They were trying to please God. Even Mormons and Muslims were trying to convert people to their way of thinking to please God. Buddhists were probably trying to please Buddha. But who would care if you became an atheist if there was no god to please? I frowned. "Why do they want you to be an atheist?"

"Atheism is how schools teach. But one thing they cannot explain."

"What's that?"

"My mother get sick, cannot work. Doctor cannot help her. Grandmother is very worried. Where do we find money for medicine? How do we live if mother do not work? Li Huo bring vegetables and cook soup for us. Other neighbors only take care of self. Li Huo pray for us. Mother get well."

"Maybe God will use your neighbor to help your parents see that Christians aren't so bad."

"This is my hope. Sunday I go to home. I want to tell parents I am Christian. I want to be baptized. I am afraid they will say no. If they do not allow me be baptized, what do I do?"

I popped another sesame ball into my mouth. "That's hard, Jason. I mean, my parents were really glad when I got baptized. I know what Chuck means. You are eighteen, but you are still living at home, on weekends anyway. You are still under your parent's authority. I think you want to do everything you can to try to get their permission. I guess you have to pray a lot about it and then tell your parents that you're a Christian and hope they will let you be baptized. Maybe they will say no at first. But you can try really hard to obey them and, you know, do what's right and stuff. Show them that you are changing now that you are a Christian."

"I must be like Li Huo?"

"Exactly. They could see how nice Li Huo was and they must have been glad for her help. Maybe if they see you make good changes they will let you be baptized."

"I guess you are right." Jason clicked his pen in and out several times. "But I am still afraid to tell them I am Christian, because I know they not be happy."

What else could I say to him? Telling his parents he wanted to be baptized would be like me telling my parents I wanted to convert to Buddhism. How could I understand what it cost Jason to live for Christ?

I got up and poured us drinks, more to fill the silence than anything else.

Jason scribbled some Chinese on a piece of scratch paper. "Daniel, I like to study Chinese proverbs. I think you must learn proverbs so you understand how Chinese people think. We Chinese say, 'Water can float a boat or sink a boat.' " He added the

English translation. "In China in old time boat is emperor. Water is people. People know that emperor must be kind to people. If people not like emperor, they make his kingdom weak."

I doodled some wavy water lines, then a floating boat and a sinking one. "I see. There's another meaning too, isn't there? Water is kind of like something hard that happens to you. It can help you or ruin you, depending on what you do with it."

"Yes. One day I have sick tooth. It hurt very bad. I try not to think about tooth, but my friend say I must go to dentist or my tooth never get well. I really hate to go to dentist, but tooth very bad, so I go. Now it does not hurt. I meet Chuck. In his office I find book about Jesus. I ask Chuck about Jesus. He invite me to come to Bible study. Now I am Christian."

"So . . . water can float a boat or sink a boat." I circled the floating boat. "Your bad tooth helped you become a Christian."

"Yes. But I think for me water like baptism too. If I be baptized, it can make me stronger Christian. But if I am afraid be baptized, if I do not tell mother and father I am Christian, I think my boat will sink. Do you understand?"

I understood—too well. Being a missionary—oops—doing God's work in China was not going to be easy. I had to look Jason in the eye and tell him his gentle grandfather was in hell. Coming from a supportive family and a strong church, I had to encourage Jason to speak out for Christ in Communist China.

I added some bubbles to the sinking boat.

My time in China could make me stronger as a Christian, or it could defeat me. After ten months in China would I return to the States floating in victory? Or would I be the one in a sinking boat?

THREE

In Seattle I did my school work, practiced the cello, and took out the trash. Mom and Dad kept the house running.

Now Mom washed the laundry and hung it on bamboo poles on the balcony. When the wind blew a sock off the pole over the edge and down five stories, it was my job to go down the stairs and rescue it.

Mom bought veggies and fruit at the market. Dad and I bought most of the rest at a large supermarket on the other side of town and taxied it home.

I also did most of the little errands near our home. I had more time than my parents and, hey, I only had ten months to experience China.

Our first Friday in China, Chuck took Dad to the university to meet Mr. Wang, his new boss. Mom was busy setting up her kitchen, so I tagged along with Dad.

Mr. Wang had a tiny office on the second floor of the administration building. He talked with Dad about teaching schedules, curriculum, and contracts. I didn't pay much attention until the end.

Then Mr. Wang turned to me. "Daniel, how do you like Huajiang?"

"It's very nice. Well, I haven't seen very much of it yet but it is . . . tall. The buildings are tall. You have a lot of skyscrapers. I am looking forward to seeing much more of it."

"Perhaps you would enjoy having a Chinese friend to show you around?"

I glanced back at Chuck. He nodded. I did too.

"My son William is seventeen years old. If you have time, he would like to have an American friend. He can show you where to find interesting things in Huajiang."

This time Chuck raised his eyebrows. He looked positive.

"Yes. Of course. I mean, that would be nice. Maybe I can meet him sometime."

Mr. Wang didn't settle for sometime. He made plans to bring William to our house the next day.

As we left the building I asked Chuck about it. "Did I say the right thing? Is it safe for me to go off with a total stranger?"

"I think you're safe enough to go with William. We know his father. Perhaps it is meant to be. When we get home, we can talk about some things."

In other words, we couldn't discuss it in public.

Chuck walked home with us to discuss Dad's contract and my new development. After a glass of cold water, some of my Chinese snacks, and a report to Mom, Chuck grinned. "Well, Daniel, it looks like you're going to be plenty busy here. You didn't expect your parents to do all the work, did you?"

"No. I've been asking the Lord to give me a job."

"Then you must be a good pray-er. You're already discipling Jason, and the Lord has brought you another Chinese friend. Maybe in time you can share the gospel with him."

"Can I do that?"

"It's time to talk about that." Chuck sat up in his chair and eyed all three of us. "We all came to China to spread the gospel. But if a Chinese unbeliever asks me why I came to China, I tell him I came to be a dentist. If an American asks me, I tell him the same thing, unless I know him very well. I did come to be a dentist. But, of course, I want to do more than that.

"If we start passing out tracts or openly saying too much about the gospel, we won't last long in China. But God brings people to us who want to learn about the Bible. People will ask you questions about spiritual things. You need to be very careful how you answer those questions. If you are too careless and bold when you speak, you endanger our ministry. More than that, your boldness can endanger Chinese believers."

I frowned. "In tenth grade I read a book about John and Betty Stam, the missionaries who were killed by Communists."

Chuck eyed me. "China has seen its share of martyrs, but remember, Daniel, the Stams lived in the 1930s. Those were very dangerous days for missionaries in China. China is constantly changing. In the 1800s Hudson Taylor had great freedom and started a great ministry. The 1900s had decades of very hard years when foreigners were not allowed in and many Chinese were martyred. But this is the twenty-first century and China is becoming more open. We don't have all the freedom we want, but we can spread the gospel if we are careful."

I studied my shoes. "But what if we do make a mistake? What will happen to us?"

"We all make mistakes and most times nothing happens. If we made a really bad mistake, the government might send us back to America and never let us return. But Chinese believers could face much worse consequences."

"Like what?" I whispered. After all we were in China. "Throw them in prison?"

"That's possible. But they would be more likely to use their jobs to punish them. There are many possibilities open to the

Public Security Bureau. So let's not force them to explore those possibilities."

Mom's eyebrows shot up. "Force them? You sound like they know about the Christian activity that's going on."

Chuck smiled. "Government officials aren't stupid. They know us foreigners are up to something. The Chinese are proud of their scenery and five thousand years of Chinese culture. But they know that few foreigners would live years in China just to see that. They know that foreigners are eager to spread their religion here and can't do that openly here. Chinese officials have got to know that many foreigners must be having Bible studies on the side. As long as we keep our activities small and hidden they will most likely leave us alone. But if we are open or obvious about it, our friends in the PSB will have to stop us to save face."

I was puzzled. "Why do they let foreigners in at all if they don't want us spreading religion?"

"China needs foreigners if they are going to modernize China. They need our expertise in areas that build their economy. They need native English speakers to teach English in order to compete in the business world."

Mom scratched her head. "So how can we spread the gospel? If someone asks us about spiritual things, how do we know if we should share what we know?"

"If someone starts asking you spiritual questions, here are three questions you need to ask yourself." Chuck raised three fingers. "Memorize these three things so you can bring them to mind at a moment's notice."

I grabbed a pen from the coffee table and wrote "1." on a dirty napkin.

He raised his index finger again. "Question one: How well do you know this person? Do you know anything about him? Is he a friend you can trust, or a friend's friend, or a total stranger? If you don't know anything about him, you need to be careful."

I scribbled that down.

Chuck raised another finger. "Question two: Does he seem to have sincere spiritual interest or is he just curious? If he is just curious or you feel he may be asking for reasons other than spiritual ones, you don't want to jeopardize your ministry by being too careless."

I added question two.

And number three. "The last question: Is this an appropriate time and place to talk about spiritual things? If not, you may need to arrange a meeting. Invite him to your house for lunch or find a place where no one can overhear you."

I wrote the third question. "But how do you know for sure? What if someone just pretends to be your friend to find out what you're doing?"

Chuck sighed. "Well, you pray a lot and ask the Lord to guide you. You will make mistakes. We all do. If you are too careful, you'll never share the gospel with anyone. So you try to be careful and go slowly. If someone shows spiritual interest, you share a little with him and see how he responds. If that goes well, you can tell him more."

That gave me lots to think about. It was hard enough to witness in America where you knew you wouldn't get in trouble for it. I came to China to witness, but I wondered if I would ever dare do it. One mistake could cost my family their future ministry. I hated to think what one mistake could cost a Chinese believer.

"Lord," I prayed. "I've got a lot of stuff I've been praying about lately. It all seems pretty important. But this one thing I want more than anything else. Please, Lord, help me never to do anything that will endanger the safety of a Chinese believer."

Our family was unusually quiet that day, thinking about all the things that Chuck had said. Later in the day Mom bought a toaster oven to join her hot plate. She celebrated by making biscuits for supper. The biscuits didn't look like her best batch. I took a bite, coughed, then gulped down a lot of water.

Dad frowned at me, then took his own bite. "I'm glad Chuck is a dentist," he said. "Looks like we might be needing one."

Mom frowned too. "I had to use a different kind of shortening and I'm not used to the toaster oven yet. They turned out a little flat, but they should be all right." Then she took a bite. She smiled. "Hmmmm. I wonder what was in that little bag I thought was baking powder."

Dad tried to look serious. "Must have got the concrete bag by mistake."

Laughter spurted out of my mouth before I could straighten out my smile. "Dad," I scolded, "You're not supposed to find fault with the food."

Dad put on his puppy dog face. "I'm sorry, dear. These are good biscuits. . . . I'm just not sure what they're good for."

Mom grinned. "We could always paint them white and use them to border that grassy circle in the courtyard."

I laughed out loud. "SOS. We could spell out SOS on the roof. Save Our Stomachs."

We all laughed then. I guess we had been a little uptight about living in China, when to share the gospel, and what would happen if we made a big mistake. Now the silliness crept in, and we laughed until we couldn't stop.

Dad wiped tears from his eyes. "You could make a bunch of little ones and sell them to a fishing tackle company for sinkers."

Mom wiped her eyes too. "I thought we came to China to be fishers of men. I never expected to go into manufacturing."

I doubled over. "Susan said she sometimes gives cooking lessons to her English students. You could teach them to make biscuits, but we might get thrown out of the country for making biscuits which are detrimental to the political interests of China. In the wrong hands these biscuits could bomb Beijing."

We laughed, far beyond reason, until we had exhausted our laughter. As the laughter left, so did the tension that had quietly been building inside of us.

"So Dad. Tomorrow William, a total stranger, is going to take me who knows where to do who knows what with who knows who."

"God."

"What?"

"God knows. Almost everything we face these days, including Mom's biscuits, are new and unknown. But God knows all about it. We just have to take it one step at a time, even if it takes us out of our comfort zone."

"What if William wants to take me somewhere I shouldn't go?"

"You take that card with our address out of your wallet, call a taxi, and come home."

"So you're just going to let me go on my own and leave it to me to use my best judgment?"

Dad sighed. His eyes held mine. "Son, your mother and I have been watching you for seventeen years. We've seen you weigh decisions and make choices. We've caught a glimpse of your heart and what you want out of life. After all that, we believe we can trust you."

I coughed. "That's it?"

"Yep."

Wow. I remembered what it felt like the first day I walked to the store by myself. I was six years old. I had to cross streets by myself. I had to pick out my own toy and bring it to the cashier and count out the money. Mom must have been pacing the floor at home, but I had bought my first toy race car all by myself. Such awesome responsibility!

Now, eleven years later, my dad was turning me loose in a foreign country with a total stranger. He wasn't giving me a lecture or a list of instructions. He just trusted me.

"Please, Lord, help me not to let my parents down," I prayed. "You either."

I wondered what I would do with a Chinese stranger the next day. As it was, William left it up to me. He and his dad showed up at our door. We walked back downstairs with his dad, who walked back to the university.

"What do you want to do?" William asked.

"What *can* we do?"

"We could go to KTV and sing songs."

Karaoke. No telling what kind of songs they would have. "Mmmmm."

"We could go shopping or go to park and play basketball. NBA is very popular in China." He held out his T-shirt with an NBA logo on it.

"Maybe not. I don't really do a lot of sports."

"We could go to internet bar and e-mail your friends in US."

I smiled. "Sure."

We walked to the closest internet bar, which sounds trendy. Really it was just a room lined with computers. William bought us Cokes and a bag of M&M's and we sat down.

"You can e-mail your girlfriend."

"I don't have a girlfriend."

"Why do you not have girlfriend?"

"I'm not really into girls. I mean, someday I'll probably want to get married and I will be very picky about the girl I choose. But I'm not ready to get married yet, so why should I have a girlfriend?"

"Do you not want to have girlfriend? Girlfriend is interesting."

"No. I'm fine without one."

"You can e-mail friend. Do you have friend?"

"I guess I could e-mail Melody."

"Is he your best friend in America?"

"No. She's a she. I mean she's a girl. And we're friends, but she's not my girlfriend. We have a weird and wonderful relationship."

"I do not understand."

"Yeah, it's hard to explain." I took a swig of Coke and ate some M&M's, but William just waited for my answer. "We're in the symphony together. She plays the violin, and I play the cello."

William looked confused.

I mimed a violinist and a cellist. "You know. Violin. Cello. We play in a big music group. We drive to practice together. We're in the same youth—" I coughed. Youth group was part of church. I couldn't talk about that. "Youth orchestra. It's the Seattle Junior Youth Symphony Orchestra. We argue a lot."

"What is argue?"

"It means, well we talk a lot, but we don't agree on anything. Actually we agree on lots of important things. We just have fun. You know . . . teasing each other. Melody's more like a sister than a girlfriend. She's a year older than I am. She starts college this year."

"What college she go to?"

Oops. How could I explain Bible college? "It's a small college in California. She studies literature. So what do I have to do to send an e-mail?"

William showed me how to get started.

"What you write your girlfriend?"

"Not my girlfriend, my friend. Melody."

"I know. What do you want to write?"

Cigarette smoke curled around my head as I sat thinking in the dark room. It was hard to write with William watching over my shoulder.

Dear Melody,
    I am here at a net bar with my new friend William. He is showing me around Huajiang. There are many tall buildings here."

My mind went blank.

"Here, William. You write something."

Dear Melody,
    I am William. Daniel is my new American friend. He say you are girl, and you are his friend, but you are not his girlfriend. I think this is very funny.

"What other things you want me write?"

"Maybe that's enough for now."

We played computer games for a while. That worked OK until a girl without a lot of clothes on popped onto the screen. We had just started the game, and I didn't want to be rude, but I wasn't eager to finish. I thought about the trust thing and decided I'd better quit while I was ahead.

"I think I'm done playing."

William's eyes grew wide. "Why? You do not like game?"

"It's not the game. It's just that, well, I don't like the way the girl on the game is dressed."

"Do you not think she is pretty?"

"It's not that. I just don't like it when . . . how can I explain it. I like girls who wear more clothes than this one."

"OK. In China boys like girls like this. I guess American boys do not."

"Well, maybe some do; but I'm an American guy, and I don't. Maybe we should go window shopping. You know, just look in stores, but not buy anything."

"I know about window shopping. We study this word when in eighth grade."

We paid the cashier and left. I was glad to get out of there, but wondered what we would do next. I hated to be picky when William was paying our way for everything, but I knew many things would push at a line I didn't want to cross.

Some of the shops had really interesting Chinese snacks, but William insisted on buying a bag of everything I asked about, so I quit asking.

We glanced through the music in the department store. William seemed disappointed when he found out I liked classical music.

We ate barbecued goat on a stick from a Chinese Muslim guy and watched him stretch long dough into noodles. So why could Muslims wear their beanies and be so open about their religion? I'd have to ask Chuck sometime.

Finally we opted for the bonsai trees at the park. They actually were pretty cool. One planter featured a tree that was growing through the middle of a rock. When William saw the sweat trickling down my face, he bought me another Coke.

"How do you think about China?" he asked.

"Well, we've been here less than a week. I haven't seen very much yet. It is really different from Seattle. I think I'll get more exercise here, going up and down the stairs. All the Chinese people I've met are nice."

"I think Seattle is very beautiful. Is it true?"

"I like it. We live in an area with a lot of trees. I will miss my ch . . . my friends. But living in China is a real adventure."

"Why do you come to China?"

I knew the answer to that one.

"My dad came to teach English."

"He teach school in America?"

"Yes. He taught math in America, too, but they only wanted him to teach English here."

"So why he does not stay in America?"

"Well, my family thought it would be interesting to live in China for a while and see what China is like."

"Are you Christian?"

I coughed. "Uh . . . yes."

William seemed unmoved by my answer. "Do you go to church?"

"Oh, you mean, the Chinese church. The one in downtown Huajiang."

"Of course. Is there another church?"

"Well, I went to church in Seattle, and I know the government has provided a church here that we could go to but, no, I don't go to it."

"Why do you not go?"

"Well, I don't know. I just, um, . . . well, I guess it's just a lot different than the church we went to in America."

"How do you know if you do not go to church in China?"

"That's just what I've heard." I needed a quick subject change here, but I couldn't think of a way to do it.

"I watch 'The Sound of Music' by Julie Andrews. Did you see that movie?"

This was better. "Yes. I think almost every American has seen it. It's a very old movie."

"Movie say Julie Andrews do not know what to do. Should she live with family and take care of children or should she work at church? She pray. Do you pray?"

"Yes."

"Does it help you?"

"Yes."

"If I pray, will it help me?"

I wanted to say that praying wouldn't help him at all because he was an unbeliever, but I couldn't say that. I hummed "The hills are alive with the sound of music," while I desperately tried to remember Chuck's three questions. "Do you really want to know about this stuff or are you just curious?"

"I am only curious. Is this bad?"

"No." I studied the next bonsai tree with unusual interest. "It's just that I'm new in China, and I'm not sure I should be talking about stuff like this in a Communist country."

"Do you not want to talk about pray?"

"I don't think so. Not now, anyway."

"I am sorry, Daniel. Do I make you angry?"

"No. I just think we'd better talk about something else."

We did then, but I was very glad to get home to our apartment on the sixth floor. I told my parents about our conversation. The next day we went to Harveys' home for supper. I gave a full report to Chuck and Susan too.

Chuck's face turned more sober than I had ever seen it. "I see. Well, you didn't really say anything bad about Communism, but do be careful, Daniel. Very few Chinese actually belong to the Communist Party—only about five per cent. Mr. Wang is one of those five per cent. I don't know how committed Mr. Wang is to the party, but if he really wanted to know what we foreigners are up to, William would make a very good spy."

FOUR

I was eating fish stomach soup when the theological question came up.

"Why do Christians not eat blood?"

Our Seattle pastor said that God is beyond time; that past, present, and future are all the same to Him. Melody and I had spent hours discussing what that meant.

If God is beyond time, did that mean that in heaven no one thing happened before another? Or does God just know about everything before it happens?

Melody and I had enjoyed passionate arguments about many theological issues, but somehow eating blood had never come up.

Max, Daisy, and Sunny had invited our family out to eat. We ordered our food. I watched to see what the Chinese Christians would do about praying. The waitress left and everything got quiet. Max offered a short but simple prayer, right out loud, and Sunny filled my soup bowl with the soup.

I sat staring at a little round fish stomach in my soup spoon when Daisy asked the question. "Chuck say Christians do not eat blood. Is it true?"

If Dad can handle a question like that, I can handle one little fish stomach, I thought, and swallowed it down. *Chewy, but not bad, actually. After the first stomach, the others in my soup would go down easier.*

Meanwhile Dad was glancing around the restaurant to see who might be listening. He set his chopsticks down. "Well, yes. I guess that's true."

"Why do Christians not eat blood?"

Dad was desperately trying to lower the volume of the whole conversation. "I imagine Chuck is thinking of the Jerusalem Council in Acts 15. I can't say that I've actually given a lot of thought to the question. Americans don't really eat much blood." He promised to think about the question and get back to her.

Daisy went on to describe some delicious blood recipes like duck's blood rice, and pig's blood soup. And we had thought since these Chinese were new Christians, they'd only ask easy questions. I could just imagine what Melody would say when I told her about it.

Sunny noticed my bowl was empty and used the clean ends of her chopsticks to add several chicken feet to my bowl. She gave me the thumbs up sign. "Chicken feet very good here."

I stared at all the little toenails reaching out to me. "Uh . . . you're going to have to help me here. I've never really eaten a chicken's foot before."

"Really? It is not hard." Sunny popped a whole foot in her mouth. As she nibbled, two of the toes slipped out of her mouth. Seconds later she spit clean bones onto her plate.

"You try to do."

I tried picking up a foot with my chopsticks, but lost hold of it.

Sunny grinned. "Use fingers."

I pushed it into my mouth. Barbecued. Chewy, but not awful. I sucked on it a little, then spit it out. The bones were far from clean.

Max noticed my embarrassment and tried to help. "Chicken feet are too hard to eat. Give him some frog legs." He used the clean ends of his chopsticks to put three in my bowl.

The first frog leg was good, but spicy. I ate one down and started on the other. Suddenly the spice kicked in and began to burn my mouth. I reached for my tea which only made it worse. Rice might have helped, but there was none on the table. I fanned my mouth.

Max smiled. "Maybe in America you don't eat much spicy food."

Sunny lifted some long, rubbery duck intestines and dropped them into my bowl. Mom was eyeing me to see if I was OK. She and Dad had been smart enough to keep their bowls full of beef and peppers and fried greens. I didn't want to offend Sunny, but she was filling my bowl faster than I could empty it. I grasped some kung pao chicken with my chopsticks and sampled it.

"The chicken is good," I told Sunny.

Sunny shook her head. "It is very standard. Not special."

"I like ordinary food. My family always eats ordinary food."

"Do you want some vegetables?" Max asked. "American food is very different to Chinese food. Maybe you don't like some of this food."

"It's good," I said. It had to be good in some sense of the word. It was nutritious, right? "But Americans don't eat feet and intestines, so I'm not very good at eating some of these things."

I started reaching out for my own food and found some of it delicious. With each serving of something I liked, I tried to gulp down a bit of the chewy intestines. As long as I ate steadily, Max and Sunny left me alone. I ate lots of noodles and totally avoided the eel. I was getting full, though it was a different full than when I ate at home. Just about the time I was wondering if dessert would come, Sunny dropped a chicken's head in my bowl.

I gazed down at the boiled head with its glassy eyes. *I don't know, Lord*, I prayed. *I think I've been doing pretty well, but I just don't think I can stomach that head even if I knew how to eat it.*

I sighed. "Whew, I'm getting pretty full."

"You must eat more," Sunny said.

Max glanced at my face. "I am full too. If I eat too much, my stomach feels uncomfortable. Anyway, we Chinese like to leave some food uneaten. If we eat everything, we think we have not ordered enough food."

I could have hugged Max. This chicken head was just going to have to go to waste.

When we got home, I grabbed a banana and searched Acts 15 again. Time to study the eating blood issue. Funny how living in another culture made you notice parts of the Bible that had been invisible before. I read some other chapters too, and began to wonder: What was church like back in Bible times?

My church in Seattle had church services down to a science. The pastors and musicians moved flawlessly from one part of the service to the next. The ushers practiced precision. If leaving your cell phone on in church wasn't the unpardonable sin, it was close. Kids weren't allowed to run in "God's house." When you were in church, you felt like you were in church.

Somehow Bible studies at Chuck and Susan's didn't feel like church at all. It made me wonder what the first churches were like.

My second Sunday in China I went to Chuck and Susan's asking God to show me what church was supposed to be like. Were all of our nice American traditions really necessary?

The group had never sung songs before. Chuck was pretty much tone deaf. But he had bought a cheap guitar for me and decided it was time to teach our group a few songs. Dad taught them the words to "God is So Good" while I played the simple chords.

Then Chuck sat on the edge of an armchair, using the coffee table as a pulpit. He talked about baptism, "the first step of obedience" for a Christian. We were planning a baptism soon, so Chuck explained our plans to fly in a Chinese pastor from another city in China to perform the baptism.

"Why don't *you* baptize us?" Max said.

Chuck leaned back in his chair. "Well, for one reason, it's illegal for foreigners to baptize people. And it just draws attention to something we need to do quietly. If the wrong people saw me baptizing, it could cause problems. I would also like to have a Chinese pastor talk to each one of you about your salvation. Each of you has good English, better than my Chinese, but I'd like to make sure you really understand what you're doing."

Sunny spoke up. "Maybe pastor from another group in Huajiang baptize us."

Were there other house churches in Huajiang? I had never thought about it before.

"If I knew a group that believed the same way we do, I would be glad to do that," Chuck said. "But I only know of a few groups. I've talked to their pastors and we disagree on some pretty important teaching. This baptism is supposed to be the beginning of a church. The church needs to go by the Bible from the very start."

"What about public church?" Sunny said. "Maybe minister from public church baptize us."

I had been wondering about the Three Self Patriotic Church ever since William asked about it. I knew that it was the official Protestant church for China. It was registered with the government, and controlled by it too. But what did this public church actually teach?

"When we first came to China, we went to the Three Self Church once, just to see what it was like. How many of you have been to the public church?" Chuck was answering a question with a question. I'd begun to recognize this as one of his strategies for getting around delicate questions.

Several said they had attended public church. Max had gone to the public church for almost a year.

"What kind of things does the minister talk about in the public church?"

Max shrugged. "The minister said we should be good neighbors, and we should treat people well. He said we must be kind to people and respect others."

Kenneth said, "Public church say must get good education, must be good citizen, and must obey law."

Chuck probed deeper. "Does the minister ever talk about the Bible?"

Max doodled on his notebook. "Every week the minister read some Bible verses. Then he closed the Bible and did not open it again. I don't think he talked about the Bible."

This was exactly the kind of thing I'd been wondering about. I should take notes. I pulled a pen and paper from our bag and wrote, "Public church—doesn't teach the Bible."

"Did the minister ever talk about Jesus?" Chuck asked.

"He said Jesus was a good man." Max started counting the points on his fingers. "Jesus taught many good things. Jesus is a good example. But he never said Jesus was God's Son or that Jesus died for our sin."

I started to write, "Jesus—not God's Son." But what was I thinking of? If I was going to carry a Bible around China, I certainly didn't want incriminating notes like this one inside. I scratched out my last note and focused on Chuck.

Chuck held out his open Bible. "A church needs to teach the Bible correctly, especially when it teaches about salvation. If a church gets salvation wrong, it really isn't a church."

"We should not go to public church?" It was Daisy this time.

"We need to choose a church carefully. In the Bible, churches were made up of true believers who checked everything they believed by the Bible. The church made its own decisions. It taught people to respect the government and obey it whenever possible. But if the government told them to do something that God said was wrong, they had to obey God. After our first group of Christians has been baptized we want this group to form our own church. We've been talking about that for a long time now."

Chuck moved on to the offering. Since a Chinese pastor was flying to Huajiang, we needed to help with expenses.

In our church in Seattle the pianist would have played an offertory, but Chuck just passed around one of Susan's Tupperware bowls.

As the bowl came around Kenneth blurted out, "What is money for? After Bible study do we eat in restaurant?"

Chuck explained it once more.

Jason rubbed a couple of coins together and looked at me. "How much money do you give?"

Time to work out my own strategy for awkward questions. I crumpled the bill in my fist and grinned. "It's my little secret."

Daisy dumped a bunch of coins into the bowl. "Can we invite friends to baptism?"

Chuck fumbled with his Bible marker. "God tells us to tell others about Jesus. Baptism is a way to show our friends we are Christians and that we want to live for God. But we must be careful too."

Susan popped the seal on the Tupperware offering bowl. "Chuck is right. Some of you have been calling on the phone and asking us what time Bible study is and talking about where we meet. When you're on the phone, that is not a good time to talk about these things. Someone may overhear who doesn't think like we do."

Chuck smiled at Susan. "Right. We need to tell our friends about Jesus, but we need to do that in a quiet way."

Daisy hung her head. "I know. But I get excited about being Christian, and I want to tell my friends."

Chuck smiled. "That's good, Daisy. But we need to be excited and careful at the same time."

She nodded. "So my friends can come to baptism?"

"Baptism is a way to show our friends we are Christians and we want to live for God. This honors God." Chuck closed his Bible and slipped it into a plain zippered case. "But not everyone in China understands why we want to be baptized. If the wrong people found out about our baptism, they could cause problems for our group. You may bring friends, but you must be sure you know your friends well enough to know that they will not cause this sort of problem."

If it was so dangerous to be a Christian in China, why were foreigners more careful than Chinese? Were we just paranoid? But if the Chinese were confusing, it was an American who really had me stumped.

Dad found a Chinese class for beginners at his university. It met three times a week, two hours each time. Since Dad taught full time and he and Mom had a full-time ministry beside, they wouldn't have time to study six hours a week. But I could go.

I looked forward to being with other foreigners in my class. I had noticed a strange thing however. As I walked around campus, other foreigners' faces stood out among the thousands of Chinese faces. As I got close to other foreigners, I would look their direction and smile. But instead of making eye contact, they always looked away, as if they didn't see me. It was spooky.

Adam, however, was friendly from the start. He sat beside me in Chinese class, which was on the eighth floor of the first building on campus. (I wondered if they put the Chinese classes in the first building so the foreigners wouldn't get lost among all the tall buildings.)

Adam and I practiced unusual Chinese sounds together. We could never get them to sound quite like our teacher, Liu Laoshi. We laughed about our problems with Chinese tones. We were sure it would be easier to teach all the Chinese English than it would be for us to learn Chinese.

Adam told me he was from Colorado. He loved to snowboard and hike in the forest. I told him I was in the youth symphony in Seattle. Adam was five years older than I was and much more athletic, but he talked to me like I was his best friend. He never swore, and with a name like Adam, I decided he must be a Christian who had come to China for the same reason I had.

Brittany sat on the other side of me. She had been in China for six months but hadn't had the time to study Chinese. She gave only the shortest answers to my questions and when I smiled at her, she hid behind her long, auburn hair and began to read.

At the end of class on our second day, Adam asked me why I had come to China. I gave him the usual My-dad's-a-teacher routine.

"I suppose you are doing some stuff on the side too." He winked.

I smiled. "Well, you know how it is."

Suddenly quiet Brittany dropped her book beside me. With it a pile of other things spilled onto the floor. Her water bottle rolled across the floor. Adam walked over to pick it up.

"Shut up!" Brittany whispered.

"Pardon me?"

"Just watch it."

I had never met anyone so rude.

Adam grabbed his Chinese book, and we headed for the door. "Now what were we talking about?"

Brittany's outburst unsettled me. I changed my answer. "Oh, yeah. While my dad is teaching in China we want to do a lot of sightseeing too."

We walked together to the university gate. I filled the time talking about some of the weird food I had eaten in China.

As I waited to cross at an intersection Brittany caught up to me. "I don't mean to be rude," she whispered. "But I know you are a friend of Chuck and Susan Harvey. I know enough about them to make some guesses about why your family is in China. In China we foreigners all have our secrets. I won't ask about yours, and you don't need to ask about mine. But I have reason to think you especially don't want to share your secrets with Adam. He has a tendency to ask dangerous questions, and I don't think he's all you think he is."

I gulped. "Thanks for warning me. I thought you were snobby, but I'm new here, and I obviously have a lot to learn. I promise you, you won't have to warn me again."

The green walk sign blinked on and I crossed the street. My heart pounded. *Thank you, Lord,* I prayed. *I hate to think what I might have told Adam if Brittany hadn't stopped me. Please keep me from making mistakes that would harm our ministry or Chinese believers.*

I might never know who Adam was or what he was doing in China, but I vowed to be far more careful in the future.

FIVE

I stepped off the curb and almost found a shortcut to heaven. A scooter whispered past, sending my shopping bag flying.

Jason rescued my bag. "Are you OK, Daniel?"

"Quiet traffic can be dangerous. Who would think that a city with nine million people would have such quiet traffic?"

Jason frowned. "Quiet is bad?"

"Sometimes quiet is good. But these electric scooters are too quiet. You don't hear them coming until they almost run over you. I've been here more than a month now. You'd think I'd be used to them."

It was Jason's turn to show me around Huajiang. He wanted me to experience "the real China." I brought my camera along so I could take pictures to send to Melody.

He took me to see a monument to Chinese inventions. He told stories of Chinese who had invented paper, gunpowder, porcelain, and the compass. His English became more broken as a quiet excitement grew in him, willing me to see the greatness of his country.

I snapped a picture of a model of the Great Wall. He pointed to the inscription in Chinese and English. "You cannot be a true hero until you have climbed on the Great Wall." His eyes glowed. "One day I will walk on Great Wall. I will be hero also." I told him I wanted to see the Great Wall, too, before I left China.

After that we walked to a Chinese music store. When Jason told the owner that I played the cello and the guitar, the owner showed me how to play the pipa (pee-paw). He said that Chinese people had been playing pipas for two thousand years. The store owner sat on a stool and held the pear-shaped pipa upright. He placed plastic picks on each finger of his right hand. Then holding the silk strings against the frets with his left hand, he plucked the strings with his right. He plucked a little tune, then got up and let me try it.

I sat on the stool and held the pipa. I adjusted my fingers as the owner patiently instructed me in a mixture of Chinese and gestures. We passed the pipa back and forth until he had taught me to play five notes. After lengthy explanations in the owner's Chinese, Jason's English, and a demonstration on a regular guitar, I thought I understood. Those five notes were a scale. The Chinese scale only has five notes unlike the Western scale with its twelve half steps.

I couldn't play "Row, Row, Row Your Boat" with those five notes, because some of the notes were missing. But I could play "Mary Had a Little Lamb" and "Amazing Grace." I learned to play a Chinese scale on a Chinese instrument with most of the instruction in Chinese! Not bad for someone who had only been a you-know-what for a little over a month. Jason snapped my picture. Melody would love this one.

Forty-five minutes after arriving I tried to express my thanks to the store owner. I nodded to him and repeated "xie xie" many times. My head ached from concentrating so hard, but I walked away with a story to write to Melody.

Jason asked me where else I wanted to go.

I was ready for this. "I want to see where you live."

"It is long way to Zhushan."

"No. Not your family's home. I want to see the dorm where you live."

Jason shrugged.

It wasn't far. In about ten minutes we walked to Jason's five-story tiled dorm building. We climbed the stairs to a crowded room on the third floor. He shared the room with three roommates. Jason used a top bunk, half of a small wardrobe, and shared a desk and chair with one of his roommates.

He pulled out the desk chair for me to sit down. "This is my room."

I sat. I had asked to see it. Now I had to find something positive to say about it. "So . . . this is your home."

"My home is in country, but I think I am very lucky God give me this room. Roommates never ask me where I go, do not care what I do. I have much freedom." Jason stomped on a cockroach. "Very clean here. Very nice."

"Can you read your Bible here?" I whispered.

Jason pulled his Bible from the top desk drawer. With the plain, black, hardback cover it could have been a dictionary. Yet every other Chinese-English bilingual Bible that I had seen looked just like this one. Several large bookmarks protruded from the top.

"Every morning I wake up and read Bible. Roommates think I am very strange. Chang Hu say 'Li Jing, why you study Bible every day? Your teachers do not give you enough books to read?'" He hugged the Bible close. "I say, 'School books help brain. Bible help heart.' He cannot understand."

Jason didn't seem to be afraid to talk about spiritual things here. Voices buzzed down the hall, but we were alone. I asked him what his parents said when they found out he had become a Christian.

"I tell parents I am Christian. They are not happy at me. I say God create world, love us, send Jesus. They say I am superstition. They say I must follow science and education." "But Christians aren't superstitious to believe what the Bible teaches. The Bible uses good science. If you study the science people use to teach evolution, that's a lot harder to believe than the Bible."

"Chuck tell me this. I do not understand everything. Always my teacher say evolution is true, evolution is fact. But Chuck say something cannot come by nothing. Beautiful world cannot come by accident. This is very hard because Chinese teachers say science prove evolution. But I know God tell truth in Bible."

"Many scientists are Christians who believe the Bible, but I don't suppose many of them live in China. Or maybe they do, but you're not going to hear much about them."

"I tell parents how can beautiful world come from explode? My heart tell me this not true. Parents say heart may say good things but must listen to heart only in secret. Only education help me get better job, help me take care of family."

Jason replaced the Bible.

I glanced down the hallway to make sure it was still empty. "So did they say you couldn't get baptized or what?"

Jason hung his head. "I am shamed, Daniel. I am afraid to ask them. But I tell them I am Christian. Maybe I ask them later."

"I will pray that you get a good chance to talk to them before the baptism."

"Thank you, Daniel. I know I must do this, but I am afraid."

"I know it's hard. Do you think they'll give you permission to be baptized?"

"I hope this. Chuck say if parents say no I should wait until next baptize and pray my parents change mind. He say God know my heart. He know I want to obey."

"Yeah. If you are trying to obey your parents, God will honor that. It's too bad it has to be so hard."

"Chinese have proverb." Jason pulled out a little pad of paper and started writing. " 'Where there is much distance to cover, you will know how good your horse is.' Baptize is hard, but maybe God want to know how good horse I am."

I studied the proverb. God was testing this new Christian, but God was testing me too. Would I adjust my life to fit cultural differences? Would I find ways to share the gospel in this difficult place? How good a horse would I be?

Jason tore off the paper with the proverb and handed it to me. "You are number three children of your parents. If you are bad son, they have another children. In China most people have one children. I am only son. If my parents think I am bad son, they do not have other son."

I couldn't imagine the pressure Jason faced as an only child in Chinese society. All of the family's expectations rested on him. It was so unfair.

"I know it's hard, Jason. I've heard about China's One Child Policy. That is so lame. How can the government tell people how many kids they can have?"

"Lame? What is lame?"

"Well, stupid. I mean, I've heard that some people have abortions when they find out they're going to have a girl. Is that right?"

Jason hung his head.

"So if every family has one boy and no girls, who will marry all the boys? People your age have no brothers and sisters, so when they have children, none of them will have aunts or uncles or cousins. That's pretty lame."

Jason frowned. "China have too many people. We must control population. Planned Birth Policy help China's problem."

"I don't mean everyone needs to have huge families, but only one child, that's a little extreme. I mean, governments have their place, but that's just too much."

Jason shook his head. "In America have big families is OK. You do not have so many people. But China is different. China have too many people."

"China is also run by Communists. That's the problem. America isn't perfect, but it was founded on Christian principles. If our government tried to start a One Child Policy, Americans would never stand for it."

"America is good country, but maybe you do not understand China yet."

One of Jason's roommates walked in then, and I wondered how loud my voice had been. Jason had spent most of his day with me, and I knew he needed to study. I told him it was time for me to go home. He walked with me down the stairs. I thanked him for spending so much time to show me around. I didn't mention the fact that he had paid for everything though I felt sure he had little spending money.

"It is honor to show teacher around Huajiang." Like I was thirty or something.

"Jason, I'd rather think of you as a friend than a student. After all, I'm younger than you are."

"You are my friend, Daniel, but you are my teacher too. You know very much about Bible. I think I am so lucky God bring you so far from America to teach me Bible."

I told him I was glad to help. I said goodbye and headed home.

The smell of tacos greeted me at the door. Taco salad was my favorite meal in China.

Thanking God for the food was easy that night. Mom had found a little shop that handmade a kind of tortilla chips especially for foreigners. The cheese was a special treat from a store that sold foreign foods. We had brought the taco seasoning with us from the States. Mom cooked the tomatoes, and the lettuce was missing because healthy foreigners had a rule about fresh fruit and vegetables. "Boil it, peel it, or forget it." Tacos weren't the easy meal they had been in the States.

I filled my plate. "Jason told his parents last weekend that he was a Christian. I don't think it went very well. Next weekend he's planning to ask them if he can be baptized. We've really got to pray for him. It's not going to be easy."

Mom broke some chips onto her plate. "We don't realize how blessed we are with Christian families to support us."

"Yeah. It's got to be hard to be a Christian here when your family doesn't support you. But Jason never complains. You should see his dorm room. He shares this little tiny room with three other guys. And he's so thankful. When I left, he told me he was *honored*—can you believe that? *Honored* to have me for a teacher. Talk about embarrassing."

Dad sprinkled cheese on his salad. "Do you ever feel like he's teaching you instead of the other way around?"

"All the time. Jason taught me another proverb today." I pulled the paper out of my pocket. " 'Where there is much distance to cover, you'll know how good your horse is.' Asking his parents if he can get baptized is hard. But he seems to see the hard stuff as a special opportunity to show God how much he loves Him. Being the only child makes it harder. We talked about the One Child Policy. I told him the Communists didn't have any right to say people could only have one child."

Dad choked on his tortilla chips and coughed to get his breath. "Daniel! Why did you say that?"

"Because they don't."

"Maybe not, but that's not exactly going to help Jason respect the government."

"Why should he respect the government when it's run by Communists?"

"Because the Bible says so. You know Romans thirteen."

I thought I did. Maybe I was wrong. "Well it talks about being subject to the higher powers. We've got to obey the government here to keep out of trouble. But we don't have to respect it, do we? I mean, we're not in America anymore. This is Communist China."

"Right. And Paul was writing to the Romans. Who do you think ruled them?"

I shrugged. "I don't know. The Roman government, I guess."

"Yeah. And when he wrote the book of Romans, Nero was their emperor. Nero was cruel from the beginning. After Paul wrote Romans, Nero killed hundreds of Christians in incredibly cruel ways."

I forked a pattern through my salad. "Weird. So why did Paul tell the early Christians to be subject to Nero?"

"Because he was the governing authority that God had appointed over them."

"Well, that's true in America, but do you really think God put the Communists in power?"

"I don't know why God allows China to have a Communist government. I do know that He allowed the present government to come to power here and that He intends to work through them. If you read your Bible, you can't get around that."

I licked spicy taco sauce off my fingers. This discussion was ruining my taco salad. "So does that mean that Chinese people can't fight for their rights?"

"If there's a legal way to do that, that's fine. But we need to do our best to live according to the laws of this government— even show respect for it. That's what honor means in the Romans passage. Since we came to China, I've read Acts over and over again."

"To see what the first churches were like?"

"Yeah. And I've practically memorized the first half of Romans thirteen. You don't read anywhere of Paul trying to overthrow the government. Acts talks a lot about Paul dealing with the Romans. He spent a fair amount of time in prison. But Acts never criticizes the Roman government or says anything bad about Roman officers. In fact, some people think Luke wrote Acts partly to defend Paul and the early church. People accused Paul of teaching people to oppose the government. But Acts shows that wasn't true. The book of Acts could have been circulated all through the Roman Empire without getting Christians into trouble."

I frowned. "Where do you get this stuff?"

"I've been reading some commentaries. I taught the book of Acts in Sunday school, and I thought I knew all about the early church until I came here. But being in China raises all kinds of new questions."

"You mean things like, 'Can Christians eat blood?' "

"Yeah. And how did the early church spread the gospel in countries whose government restricted it? When should we be bold, and when should we be careful?"

"So now you have it all figured out?"

Dad laughed. "Oh no. I'm still trying to sort out what part of my thinking is biblical and what part is just American. I have a long way to go. We might not like some of China's rules, but God didn't bring us to China to criticize the government and its policies."

"So I blew it."

"I'd say so."

"Oops."

"It's hard enough for these people to be subject to the authorities without mission—well, you know, Christians inflaming them to rebel. We need to help them obey the law whenever they can do that without disobeying God."

Was I really *inflaming Jason to rebel?* I was pouring my life into Jason, trying to help him. Was I hurting him instead?

I sighed. "I'm no good at this discipling stuff."

"That's not true, Daniel. You just made a mistake. I imagine we'll all make plenty. We just have to be sure to learn from our mistakes. God can still use us, but we have to be careful."

Right. Make a mistake in America and someone laughs at you. Make a mistake in China and you bring serious trouble to your best friends. Why did it have to be so hard?

I stacked my silverware and napkin and glass on my plate to carry them to the kitchen. Washing the dishes was my part of the family chores. I only wished my discipling job was as easy as the dishes.

"Dad, do you ever think about what you would say if we get caught."

"You mean, what would I do if our friends at the Public Security Bureau find out that we're doing Bible studies?"

"Yeah."

"We'll pray they don't."

"But what if they do? What if they ask you about what you do when you're not teaching English?"

"I guess I'll give them vague answers."

"What if that doesn't work? What if they ask you questions that endanger our ministry or put Chinese believers at risk? Would you lie to protect them?"

"I wouldn't necessarily tell them everything I know, but it wouldn't be right to lie."

"So what if they ask you straight out if you've ever had a Bible study in China? What if they ask you if you've ever told a Chinese person how to become a Christian? What would you say then?"

Dad scraped up the last of his taco salad. I could hardly hear his answer. "I don't know."

SIX

My three-year-old niece, "Blabby Abby," never stopped talking. Tuning her out saved my sanity—until she discovered the question "Why?"

William, at eighteen, was China's answer to Blabby Abby.

"Do you like China? Are you homesick for America? What kind of food do you eat in America? Do you go to Disneyland? In America is every person Christian? Does every person go to church? Why do people go to church?"

I really shocked him when I told him I didn't go to a school in China, that I was homeschooled.

"Is your mother your teacher? Do you make good grades? How long time do you study every day? Is your school good enough? How do you hope to get into university if your school is your home?"

I decided William's questions were good practice for living in China. But questions could be dangerous. I hadn't forgotten Chuck's comment that William would make a good spy.

William had taken me to karaoke, to his home to watch NBA basketball, to see a Chinese acrobatic show, to lots of stores. So on National Day in October I invited him for lunch at our apartment.

Before he came, I stuffed our Bibles and Christian books in the bookcase. It wasn't illegal for us to own Bibles and read them for ourselves, but I didn't exactly want to flaunt them.

I closed the calendar and put it in the cupboard. William didn't need to see the names of people we did personal Bible studies with.

I eyed the posters on my bedroom wall. A Great Wall poster hung over my bed. Beside it I had hung the picture of the Great Wall model I had visited with Jason and the famous Great Wall saying. "You cannot be a true hero until you have climbed on the Great Wall." No problem with this.

I turned to the other poster. "In all thy ways acknowledge Him and He shall direct thy paths." William wouldn't know it was a Bible verse, but, like Blabby Abby, he might ask about it. I pulled it down.

How could I fill the afternoon with something besides questions? I decided to buy a Chinese game called "Go." I had seen old men sitting on little stools by the street playing this game. Once I saw some kids playing it too. It looked about like checkers, so I figured it couldn't be too hard. I raced to the store and back.

I had just opened the game board when I heard William's footsteps echoing in the stairwell. He rang the bell, and I invited him in. He had never seen much of the inside of our house before, so he glanced at all the furnishings.

"Your house is very American."

I frowned. "What do you mean? It is a Chinese house built by Chinese people in China. We bought our furniture here too."

William pointed to the family pictures on the wall. "I think Americans like many pictures on wall. They like pictures of family. You buy furniture in China, but it is American-style Chinese furniture. Refrigerator is in kitchen, not in living room. You have oven. Chinese people do not have oven."

It was just a toaster oven, but it was the biggest they had at the department store.

"My mom likes to bake cookies and cakes. It saves a lot of money."

William strolled over to the window and rubbed the drapes between his fingers. "Your mother make curtains too?"

"Well, yes. She knows how to sew, and she knows how she wants the house to look, so it's just easier to sew them herself."

"We Chinese buy bread and cake at bakery. We pay tailor to make curtains, give job to Chinese people."

You'd think it was against the labor laws to do things for yourself.

I showed him my bedroom and explained some things about homeschooling.

He checked the brand on my laptop. "Your parents have a computer, and you have one too. I think you are very lucky."

"I need my computer for my schooling. I will use it in America when I go back for college too. My parents paid half of the money for it, and I earned the other half at Pizza Hut."

William raised his eyebrows. "You work and go to school too?"

"I did in America. A lot of high school students have jobs."

William shook his head. "I do not understand Americans. In China school is very important. Always we study. How can American students get time to work and study at school too?"

"Uh, I don't know. I guess we're just not as good students as you are here in China."

We sat down to what I realized was a very American lunch. Tuna sandwiches, potato chips, and Coke to drink—with ice. Chinese often drank their coke warm, but never with ice. After all, to make ice cubes you had to boil the water, then cool it, then freeze it. Mom rationed out three ice cubes for every drink.

I felt so American, which wasn't fair. I tried to be a friend to William and invited him to lunch. I wanted to win him to Christ, yet I had to hide my Christianity at the same time. After all that I felt guilty for being an American, like I had a choice.

Mom passed the food. My family fumbled with their napkins. William seemed to notice. "My friend say Christians always pray when they eat. Is it true?"

Dad nodded. "Yes."

"So you must pray. I want to see what Christians do."

We closed our eyes. Dad prayed, "Father in heaven, we thank you for making the world for us to live in and for giving us food to eat. Amen."

It must have been the shortest prayer Dad had ever prayed.

Mom and Dad asked William about his school. He asked Mom how she knew what to teach me for homeschool. She pulled out some of my nice, safe math curriculum.

William thumbed through it. "Is it hard to teach Daniel?"

Mom smiled. "No. Daniel is a good student. He works hard and gets good grades. That makes it very easy to teach him."

William frowned. "If he is a good student, maybe he will go to Harvard or MIT?"

Dad shrugged. "I don't think Daniel wants to go to Harvard or MIT. We don't care if Daniel goes to a top university or even gets a job that makes a lot of money. We want him to do his best and learn skills so he can get a job. We want Daniel to be happy and find something that he's good at doing and enjoys doing. We want him to use his life well, to be kind and caring to other people."

"It does not matter if Daniel get high education, if he get job that pay much money?"

"No. If he makes enough money to live on and support whatever family he has, that's good enough."

William shook his head. "American thinking is very strange."

Mom cleared the table, and Dad went back to his room to study.

"Daniel, I know it is not American culture to ask how much money your father make."

"That's right. Americans usually consider that kind of question too personal to ask."

William grinned. "But we have a Chinese saying, 'Follow the local custom when you go to a foreign place.' "

"In America we say, 'when in Rome, do as the Romans do.' "

"I must write American saying so I do not forget." William sorted through his backpack and came back with a notebook and pen. He made me write the words in English. "Yes, when in Rome, do as Romans do. In China we ask these questions. So I am curious. My father work with English teachers in China, but in America how much money does your father make?"

I matched his grin. "That's our little secret." I pulled out the Go game. "Can you teach me to play Go?"

William shrugged. "I can teach you to begin Go. You must use whole life become master."

"Really? I see people playing it all the time on the streets. It doesn't look hard."

William set up the board. He gave me the markers that looked like black M&M's and took the white ones for himself. He showed me how to capture a stone, then how to capture a group of stones. I learned enough to play a simple game. That ate up forty-five minutes. The game made me sleepy—and less careful.

"Chinese play Go more than three thousand years. Confucius say if people play Go they waste time, but Chairman Mao make all generals study it. During time of Cultural Revolution government does not like Go, but today, it is very popular."

I frowned. "So do Communists today like the game or not?"

William shrugged. "It does not matter. Today we Chinese have freedom. It does not matter if we play Go or we do not play Go."

I took a cookie from the plate. A Chinese baker could have earned a third of a yuan from this cookie, and I was cheating him out of it.

William lowered his voice. "Daniel, my friend say Americans do not like Communist. Is it true?"

I coughed. "I don't know. Some do and some don't, I guess. It's not really something that concerns most Americans."

"But you do not like Communist?"

How would Chinese answer this? "I think we Americans don't understand Communism very well."

"You are Christian," William whispered. "In America, Christian is good, but in China, no. I think Communist Party is path to success. My father say join Communist Party is big advantage, help me in many ways. But Christian thinking, Communist thinking, they are not the same."

I whispered back. "Are you a Communist Party member?"

"Not yet. When I become eighteen, my father say it is time to join Party, but I do not join yet. Right now I am very busy. May 21 I become nineteen. I think before I am nineteen, I will join Party."

I gulped. Did I dare ask one more question? "Are Communist Party members ever Christians?"

William shook his head. I could hardly hear his answer. "Communist say Christian is not good. Christian is superstition."

"I guess Americans think each person should be able to believe whatever he thinks is right."

"It does not matter what person think—what person believe. He must lock inside. It is secret." William grinned. "Like how much money your father make. But I think I must join Party or never success."

So William hid secrets too.

That night I lay in bed thinking about our talk. After months of zipping my lip, how could I be such an idiot? William was my friend. We had talked about all kinds of cultural issues. William loved to hear me talk about America. But I must never forget that William's parents were Party members, and he would be one soon. I would have to save my difficult questions for Jason. I knew I could trust him.

My next project was English corner. Mr. Wang had been pressuring Dad and the other teachers to do more English corners. This gave students a chance to practice their English by asking foreigners questions in English and listening to the answers.

Dad stretched his time to teach university classes, then teach Bible studies and learn Chinese on the side. But he needed to please Mr. Wang too. Some of the students had come back early from their National Day holiday for make-up classes. Mr. Wang thought it would be a good time for an English corner. He suggested that Dad bring me along. We could do two favors for the price of one.

Jason called from his home in the country to ask me how my holiday was going. I told him about the English corner and asked him to "think" about me. He assured me that he would "pray" for me. I was trying to teach Jason be more careful over the phone, but he often slipped. I should have known better than to mention it.

English corner at this university was some stools in the back of a dark bookstore. Dad said last time only a few students had shown up. Dad told me that I could answer most questions. I just had to remember that this place was too public to witness. If someone asked questions about Christianity, I should give general answers and change the subject. Anything deeper than that needed to be answered in private.

It didn't sound too hard.

Just before eight, Dad and I arrived at the bookstore. We found a couple of students hanging around and chatted with them. They asked Dad how long we had lived in China and if we liked it.

Soon a couple more students crept up and asked me how old I was and how many brothers and sisters I had.

Then a nearby class finished and students flooded the bookstore.

Two giggly girls edged in close to me.

"How old are you? Do you have girlfriend? Would you like Chinese girlfriend? In marriage, what is most important—love, parents' wishes, or money?"

I told them that I was too young to get married and didn't know much about it. This brought hysterical giggles.

A cluster of guys crowded around.

"Do you know Chinese? How much money do you make? How much money does your father make?"

That again. I was glad I didn't know the answer. Students surrounded Dad until I couldn't even see him anymore.

The subject in my group changed to hobbies, and my mind raced to give some sort of rational answer to all the questions.

"What is it like to study in America? My teacher say Americans own guns. Is it right?"

I remembered something Chuck had told me. "When you don't know what else to say, praise China."

I told them how the music store man taught me to play the pipa. I talked about my dream to see the Great Wall someday. I asked the students questions, but no one wanted to hear their answers. Foreigners were so much more interesting than other Chinese. Thankfully this American was wearing deodorant. The students crowded around me had clearly never heard of it.

Then I spotted a familiar face. William had come, either to support me or watch me squirm. He squeezed through the crowd.

I grabbed his arm. "This is William. He is my friend." I recited some of the places William had taken me and what we had done together.

"How did you become William's friend?" It was the outspoken guy who was asking most of the questions.

I told him about my dad's job and Mr. Wang. William was enjoying his honored role, but people soon ran out of questions to ask about our friendship.

William grinned. "Daniel is Christian. Many Americans are Christian."

I gulped. Chinese eyes warmed with interest.

"My teacher say Christians follow Jesus. Who is Jesus? Is Jesus a man or a woman? How old is He?"

I peeked over shoulders to see Dad, but he was seated below a sea of black heads.

"Christians believe Jesus is God's Son. He came to earth about two thousand years ago. Americans celebrate His birth at Christmas. He was born into a poor family. They were traveling when he was born, and the inns, like hotels, were full so he was born in a stable where they usually kept animals."

"So who is Santa Claus? Is he Jesus' brother?"

I pulled the hanky from my pocket and mopped sweat from my face. Santa was safer than Jesus. I could tell them lots about Santa. I was just getting to the elves and the reindeer when I spotted Jason near the back of my group. He smiled. He must have come back early from his holiday for the Sunday morning Bible study.

"Why do Americans talk about God so much?" It was William again, showing off, I thought. "In American movies people pray. They go to church. I saw American Christmas movie. Children act plays and Jesus is baby. They have donkey and sheep and camel. Why do they think God is so important?"

I glanced at my watch. Nine o'clock. Dad had told me that English corner would never end if you didn't make plans to leave and do it. Tonight Mom was expecting us home at 9:15.

"We have to go now. Someone is expecting us at 9:15."

I stood on tiptoe. Dad was standing now. His receding hairline showed over the heads of shorter Chinese.

"Hey, Dad, gotta go!" I yelled.

He made apologies and wiggled through the crowd. Jason and William joined us outside the bookstore. My heart was thumping, but I kept it light.

"Hi, Jason. When did you get here?"

"Fifteen minutes before. I come back to school from home, think about you at English corner. I think I must visit my friend, listen to you answer. Do you like English corner?"

"It went all right. Jason, this is my friend William."

Jason nodded. "I know Wang Ping. He is my classmate."

"Li Jing, how do you know Daniel?" William asked.

"When Daniel come to China, I find out he is Christian. I think he will want to have Christian friend. He teach me—"

"I teach him and he teaches me," I broke in. "I teach him Chinese, and he teaches me English. No. Wait. It's the other way around. You know. He wants to practice his English just like you do." I brushed a trickle of sweat from my brow.

Dad rescued me from my panicky attempt to cover Jason's remark. "Jason has been teaching Daniel about Chinese culture. Jason is Daniel's friend the same way you are his friend."

William nodded. We left him to wait at his bus stop.

When we were well out of William's hearing range I said, "Jason, why did you tell William that we were Christians?"

Jason frowned in confusion. "He already know you are Christian. I think I must tell him I am Christian too. Maybe William will want to be Christian like us."

"I hope William will become a Christian . . . some day. I want him to get saved as much as you do. But we must be careful. If he found out about our Bible study group and told the wrong people, it could cause all kinds of trouble. If we want to keep studying the Bible, we've got to be careful who we tell about these things."

We had reached Jason's bus stop. He stood silently for a few moments, letting my words sink in.

I searched his face. "Do you understand what I mean?"

He nodded. "I think I understand most of your words, but one part I do not understand."

"What's that?"

"This week I read Romans. I read Christians are not ashamed of gospel of Christ. But you say, 'Be careful.' Careful . . . ashamed. What is difference?"

SEVEN

Jason's question made me take a good look at what I was doing in China. I didn't want to endanger a Chinese believer, but maybe I was being too careful. Would I ever be able to tell an unsaved person about the gospel?

My family talked about it and prayed for opportunities to witness. My opportunity came just a day and a half after English corner.

Adam and some of the European students had ended their National Day holiday with a big party the night before. They came to Chinese class with serious hangovers. They repeated the vocabulary words with the rest of us, but their pronunciation was worse than usual.

We were discussing healthy diets. *"Wo shi chi su de,"* meant "I am a vegetable eater—a vegetarian."

"Some people are vegetarians for their belief," the book said in Chinese and English. "But some people eat a vegetarian diet for their health."

Belief. In this context it meant religious belief. An interesting word for a Chinese book in China. Belief was one of those words we locked inside of us. It was not an illegal word, but it raised questions. Liu Laoshi taught us how to ask, *"Do you have a belief?"* in Chinese. And how to say *"Christian, Jew, Buddhist, Muslim, atheist."*

Did Liu Laoshi know what she was doing, teaching us all these risky words? We had practiced stuffing these words inside of us like an overstuffed suitcase. Now that the lid had cracked open and the words had come out, would they ever go back again?

We took turns asking each other in Chinese, "Do you have a belief?"

Most of the Europeans answered, "No. I have no belief." One said, "I am a Protestant, but I don't believe in God."

"Do you have a belief?" I asked Adam in Chinese.

"No," he said, "I am an athiest. Wu Dan, do you have a belief?"

I glanced at Liu Laoshi who stood beside us, waiting for the answer. "Yes. I have a belief. I am a Christian."

It felt really strange saying that in public in China. I had to remind myself that it was legal to be a Christian in China. I could say this. Government officials would expect most foreigners to have some sort of religion.

Several Americans, including Brittany, echoed my words. But I could see the M-word flashing in Adam's eyes. Every Christian suddenly smelled suspiciously like a missionary. Adam wouldn't forget that.

When break came, you could tell the Christians by the way they suddenly changed the subject. The ones who had publicly declared they were Christians—the ones I suspected of being Ms—immediately started making small talk about anything except religion. Two European students lay their heads on their desks, nursing hangovers from the party the night before. Adam headed for the restroom.

Liu Laoshi wandered over to talk to Brittany and me. She often used the breaks to help us practice our Chinese.

"Today some of our students don't feel comfortable." She kept her Chinese words simple. She glanced at the hung-over students. "You two are feeling well?"

I nodded. "Very well, Laoshi."

"Maybe some students on holiday *he jiu, he tai duo.*"

I frowned. "Sorry. I don't understand."

"He jiu, he tai duo, means 'drink too much wine.' You two do not drink wine?"

Brittany (Chen Bai) shook her head. "No. I do not drink wine."

"Wu Dan, I think you are too young to drink wine."

"Yes, Laoshi, I am young. But I do not want to drink wine." I grinned. "To learn Chinese I need to think clearly."

She smiled. "Yes, For Americans to learn Chinese, it is not easy. Do you get up early to study Chinese?"

"In the morning I get up at 6:15, but I do not study Chinese."

"Why do you get up so early?"

I looked confused, so she repeated the question in English.

Now I felt the heat. "I read . . ." *Careful . . . ashamed . . . what is the difference? Should I say more?* I glanced at Brittany. She nodded. "I read the Bible."

"Really? You do? Wow, you are a diligent Christian." She turned to Brittany. "Chen Bai, do you read the Bible too?"

"Yes, in the morning I read the Bible too."

Liu Laoshi glanced back at me. "After you read the Bible, what do you do?"

"My family eats breakfast." I pulled out my hanky and mopped my forehead. "Then my whole family reads the Bible together."

"Really? Do you like reading the Bible?"

"Yes. I like reading the Bible very much."

"I think Christians are good people. They don't do bad things. I also have read the Bible."

"Really? What part did you read?" asked Brittany.

"Genesis."

I said, "Genesis is a very interesting book."

"Yes." Liu Laoshi turned as Adam's footsteps came closer. "Wu Dan, Chen Bai, your Chinese is improving. You are good students. But it is time to start class now."

I arched my eyebrows at Brittany as we took our seats. Liu Laoshi taught us Chinese words for eating in restaurants, but my mind was going over Chuck's three questions. We had said quite a bit to our teacher about the Bible in a fairly public place. Brittany hadn't tried to change the subject either.

How well did we know Liu Laoshi? She had taught us for nearly a month and a half, and these were her first remarks about spiritual things. That didn't sound like a trap.

Was she sincerely interested in spiritual things? She could be simply curious, but she had read the whole book of Genesis.

Appropriate time and place? The Public Security Bureau didn't care much if foreigners converted each other. Liu Laoshi had been the only Chinese person in the room. The only other people within hearing range were ones who claimed to be Christians.

I decided God had answered our prayers and given us this opportunity to begin to witness to our teacher.

But one thing scared me in Chinese class—Adam.

At first I thought Brittany must be wrong about Adam. Friendly and polite, he seemed to be a shining example of all my parents taught me to be. Everyone loved him. When I walked across campus with Adam, faces lit up and girls giggled.

People stared at me too, because I was a foreigner, but they were definitely less interested when Adam wasn't beside me. Was I jealous?

Actually not everyone loved Adam, but certain people lit up when he was around. Mr. Wei, the head of the English department. Ms. Li, who handled visa issues. Sam Yang, head of the student body. Mickey Zhang, who wore designer clothes and owned her own car. Peter Qiu, who always talked about the greatness of the Communist Party. Power people loved Adam.

I was the last rung on the power ladder. So why would Mr. Personality care about a seventeen-year-old cello wimp? Somehow all the flattery and good buddy status didn't ring true.

I couldn't be rude, so I handled Adam with my gift of gab. Between classes I collected all the quirky things that happened to me in China. I worked them into a mindless monologue. When I saw Adam, I rattled on endlessly about weird food I'd eaten, strange things I'd seen, and funny encounters with people. That left no time for dangerous questions.

After I learned to do that, Chinese class was easy.

Dealing with William, however, was getting difficult. The next time I saw him, he asked all kinds of questions about Jason. He asked how often we got together, where we went, and what we studied. Not good.

I had met with William about every week so far, but I started making it every other week. I shortened my time with him and tried to do activities which would keep us busy doing things and give us less time to talk.

"Please, Lord," I prayed. "Help me not to say anything to William that would endanger Jason's safety. And keep the believers in our little group safe."

Jason and I finished up the new believer's Bible studies. We still met once a week. Jason always had Bible questions that he was wondering about, and I tried to answer them.

He kept asking me to pray that he would have the courage to ask his parents if he could get baptized. Weeks went by. Every day my family prayed for him. When he finally asked his parents, they didn't say yes, but they didn't say no either. I told Jason that was a good sign.

I'll never forget the time he asked me what heaven was like. I turned to Revelation 21 and 22. I talked about gates made from huge pearls and transparent gold streets. I showed him in his English-Chinese Bible the names of all the jewels in the foundation. Then I skimmed down to the part about the crystal-clear river and the tree of life. I've never been sure how the tree of life could bear a different kind of fruit every month in a place that had no sun or moon to mark the time. I glanced up to explain this to Jason.

His face shone like a kid with a new toy. "Wow! Heaven is very beautiful! God is so good! He give us His Son Jesus and heaven too! Christians are so lucky!"

Well, Christians don't believe in luck. But I wasn't about to correct Jason. I never saw an American's face light up like that about heaven. I had grown used to hearing about heaven. I was more interested in the fruit-bearing cycle of its trees than the goodness of God. I needed some of Jason's spiritual enthusiasm.

My family grew more and more comfortable living in China. Every other week Dad and I rode the bus to a large German supermarket. Loading our shopping cart high, we bought more in this one store than we could get in many stores in our area. Between us we worked out a way to get armloads of groceries into a taxi and up five flights of stairs.

Mom invented lots of American recipes out of Chinese ingredients, studied the Bible with Chinese ladies, and learned Chinese.

Dad taught English and Bible studies and learned Chinese.

I basked in my freedom. Even with a light homeschool schedule for my senior year, Chinese three times a week, William, Jason and group Bible studies, I had time left over to explore Huajiang.

For several weeks I checked out every bike shop in the area. Finally I bought a sturdy blue bike with a wire basket and a lock and chain. It was a practical bike more than a racer, but it brought me new freedom.

Melody had been begging me for pictures. For her birthday in November I decided to send her a CD of pictures from my new life in China. Every day I'd strap my camera around my neck, unlock my bike from the apartment bike stand, and hunt for pictures.

The first week was food week. On day one I took pictures of every kind of fruit I could find—the normal ones plus lichees, dragon eyes and dragon fruit, and foul-smelling, spiny durian. On veggie day I counted how many new veggies I could photograph at the market. I brought home some fresh green soybeans for Mom to stir-fry with chicken.

When Jason came for Bible study I couldn't help bragging. "See what I found in the market?"

"*Mao dou* is one Chinese name for it. It means, 'hair beans.' Outside shell is very hairy."

"Well in English we call them soybeans. Melody's mom calls them edamame and pays a lot for them. But I bought a jin in the market for two yuan!"

"I think that is price for foreigner. If you are Chinese, vegetable seller charge you much less money. You can buy two jin for two yuan."

I folded my arms. "She cheated me?"

Jason shrugged. "Maybe not cheat, but charge too much, yes."

I grunted in disgust. "I've been buying a lot of things at the market or little stores that don't mark the price. I wonder how many people have been cheating me."

"You ask price?"

"Yes."

"You want to buy things? You pay price?"

"Yes."

"This is not cheat. This is charge too much."

The more I thought about it, the more this annoyed me. Charging me more for being a foreigner just wasn't fair. But I couldn't change it, so I tried to forget about it and find more pictures.

On bread and noodle day I found steamed buns, dumplings, noodles, and flat round bread. I sneaked into little bakeries to snap quick photos of Chinese pastries. During transportation week I shot pictures of every kind of old and new three-wheeled car I could find plus bikes, scooters, cars, buses, and trains. I even found an ancient cart pulled by a horse.

By the third week I was really getting to know my way around Huajiang. Time for a little culture.

I hunted up the music store where I played the pipa. The owner grinned when I walked in. I held up my camera and tried to explain what I wanted. He pointed out the various instruments, rattling away in Chinese while I clicked the shutter. He showed me how to play each one while he was at it. I should have brought a video camera. It took almost an hour, but I knew Melody would love the pictures.

On my way to Chinese class I found a student writing Chinese calligraphy with a waist-high calligraphy brush and muddy water on the sidewalk. That set me searching for cool examples of Chinese calligraphy. That afternoon I spotted some awesome scrolls in a promising little store on the main street. The bamboo drawings blended perfectly with the Chinese calligraphy. Melody loved calligraphy, even in English.

I couldn't read the Chinese characters, but some scrolls had English on them, for tourists I supposed. "A great man can bend and stretch." Appropriate with the bamboo pictures. "In all thy ways acknowledge Him . . ." It was Proverbs 3:5 and 6! Other scrolls had John 3:16 and John 14:6! My heart thumped harder. Here I stood on a main street in China staring into the main shop window, and I could see three Bible verses on display! Maybe China *was* becoming more open. My shutter finger itched, but I didn't want to make the shop owner nervous.

I slipped inside the store. A bell tinkled and a friendly Chinese lady appeared from the back room. She greeted me in Chinese. I pointed to the scrolls with Bible verses. "Very beautiful. Very interesting." I said in Chinese. "How much?"

She named a price. I had to buy a Bible scroll for Melody. "*Hau*," I said. Good. I would buy it. I wanted to ask her if she was a Christian. I wanted to tell her that I was a Christian too, and that it warmed my heart to see a Bible verse publicly displayed in China. But what would that accomplish? I wanted the lady to feel safe with me. So I just kept smiling and nodding at her and thanking her.

I hid my purchase inside my backpack and headed for the park where William had taken me. I got pictures of the bonsai tree and rock sculptures and some scenes of ancient figures carved into stone.

I snapped pictures of the stone scenes of ancient children playing games. Melody would love these pictures. Tonight I would burn a CD of them to send to her, and another CD to keep for our family. Mom could choose the best ones for a China scrapbook. I couldn't help grinning at my camera full of pictures. It was worth the three weeks it took to get them.

I returned to the stand where I had locked my bike. The first rusty stand I approached was full of bikes, but none like mine. I checked the other stands nearby. No shiny blue bike. The longer I searched, the more frantic I became. What had happened to my bike? As I returned to the first stand for the third time, I discovered a chain and lock on the ground. One link of the chain had been cut through. Someone had stolen my bike!

I grabbed the lock and chain and stuffed it into my backpack. A Chinese lady walked to the rack and fingered the combination of her lock. She glanced at me. I wanted to say, "Some idiot stole my bike! He had no right to do that! I made sure I locked it and everything!" But I didn't know the lady and I didn't know how to say all that in Chinese. She pulled out her bike and rode away.

I kicked the bike stand. What now? Should I leave the scene of the crime? I didn't think there was much hope of getting my bike back, but if I left now, there would be no hope at all.

I dialed Jason on my cell phone. "Jason, I am by the park with the Chinese statues in it. I came back to get my bike, and it's stolen! Someone cut the chain!"

"I am sorry, Daniel."

"What should I do?"

"Get a pedicab."

"But my bike? How can I get my bike back?"

"I think it is impossible, Daniel."

"But it's so unfair! I locked it and everything! It's a brand new bike!"

"Buy new bike is not good. People like to steal new bike. Must buy old bike. If no dirt, people will steal."

"You mean I'm supposed to buy a rusty old bike just so it won't get stolen?"

"It is good idea."

"But I don't want to ride a rusty old bike around."

"No one like old bike. That is why old bike is best bike. No one steal."

I sighed. "Well, should I call the police or something?"

"Stolen bikes are like cockroaches."

"What?"

"So many cockroaches. So many stolen bikes. Police cannot do impossible job."

I wanted to strangle Jason just then, but it wasn't his fault. What did I expect in a country of over a billion people with half as many bicycles?

I took Jason's advice and stopped a three-wheeled car. Actually I turned down the first two pedicabs that came my way. They were old, dirty ones with pedal power. Tonight I would ride in a shiny, new, motorized three-wheeled car that was completely enclosed if I had to wait all night for one.

That made me late for supper, but Mom was too sorry for me to scold. After that I called Uncle Chuck to complain.

He laughed. "Well now you're a real M," he said.

"What?" A real missionary?

"You're not a real M until you've had your bicycle stolen."

I had expected sympathy from Chuck, but I wasn't going to get any. I decided Chuck had lived in China too long if a stolen bike didn't make him mad.

I was too angry to download the pictures that night. But as I walked home from Chinese class the next day, I spotted another good picture to add to the ones I had taken. It was the office of the police station. I was still disappointed that the police couldn't help me find my bicycle, but I had to admit that it wouldn't be easy to manage more than a billion people.

I lifted my camera and took a picture of the sign. I clicked another one for good measure. But the angle was all wrong. I needed to get the building too. I moved over to the curb and took a few more pictures. Hmmm. I never noticed how interesting the police station was. Tiny tiles formed a clever mosaic on the side of the building. And I really should get a picture of the statue in front. A concrete mother and father lifted a concrete little boy high above them. The classic symbol of the One Child Policy. I had to get that.

The shutter clicked time after time. After three weeks of snapping pictures my memory card must be nearly full. I wondered if I would run out of room.

Clouds darkened the sky, but they couldn't darken my enthusiasm.

Then a hand gripped my shoulder. I turned to face the olive green uniform of a Chinese policeman. He was not smiling.

"Come." he said. He nodded toward the police station. It wasn't a place I would choose to go, but this was one time I didn't have a choice.

EIGHT

Inside the building our footsteps echoed down a very long hallway and into a smoke-filled room. Whispers hissed between various officers. One whispered a phone conversation.

The door swung open and yet another officer strode in. He stepped up to my chair, nodded politely, smiled. "I speak English. I will be your translator. You will come with me please."

I followed him down a maze of hallways and up several flights of stairs to an air-conditioned room. He seated me on a well-worn chair and brought me a cup of tea. "You will wait, please," he said and disappeared through another door.

Several minutes later the translator returned with an older officer with stripes on his sleeve. The older officer rattled off quick Chinese, and the translator did his job. "May we see your passport please?"

"I, uh, I didn't bring it with me. It doesn't really fit in my pocket very well. I'm sorry. I know, I should carry it with me. I will after this. Really."

"What is your name please?"

"Daniel Wheeler. Wu Dan is my Chinese name."

He jotted notes in a small notebook. "What are you doing in China, Daniel?"

I told him that my dad taught English at the university.

"May we see your camera, please?"

I pulled the strap from around my neck and handed it to him. The translator handed it to the older officer, who strode from the room. How many months had I washed dishes at Pizza Hut to buy that camera?

"I was just taking pictures to send back to my friend in America," I told the translator. "The mosaic picture on the side of this building is very interesting. Also the statue out front. You know, the mother and father and child. Well, it makes a nice family picture. We like families. We believe in families." I decided I'd better shut up before I told him that the family was ordained by God.

He lit a cigarette. "You took very many pictures."

"Well, yes. I've been taking lots of pictures. Pictures of fruit and vegetables and bonsai trees. You can look on my camera. It's all there."

"Yes. They will look at your pictures."

"Am I in trouble or something? I didn't mean to do anything wrong. I mean, I'm only in China for ten months. You have a very beautiful country, and I want to take pictures to show to my friends. I didn't think there was a law against that. No one seemed to mind when I took pictures of vegetables. All tourists take pictures, don't they?"

He leaned on a desk and puffed his cigarette. "All tourists take pictures. Not many take pictures of vegetables, I think. But do not worry. In China we are very reasonable. We do not prosecute people for photographing vegetables. Mr. Wu will return your camera."

"The officer's name is Wu? My name is Wu too. I mean, I know we're not related or anything. We just chose Wu as a Chinese surname because it sounds a little like Wheeler."

The translator stubbed out his cigarette, reached for my dirty teacup and left the room. Perhaps this was a sign that I should shut up. I mopped the sweat from my neck and forehead and sent up some frantic prayers. In the background the secretary carried on jerky phone conversations. Thirty minutes ticked by until the translator marched in with Mr. Wu.

With stiff politeness Mr. Wu questioned me about the two months I had spent in China. Why was I here? How long would I stay? What did I do with my time? Who were my friends? How did I meet them? Why did I want to know Chinese?

Only later did I think about the questions he *didn't* ask me. What did I do on Sunday? Have I ever tried to convert a Chinese person to Christianity? Have I ever gone to a house church?

After nearly an hour of questioning Mr. Wu and the translator drove me back home. My wide-eyed parents met us at the door.

I ran to get my passport and handed it to Mr. Wu. He thumbed through it and handed it back with my camera. He nodded a crisp salute.

Mr. Wu mumbled something and the translator said, "Sorry to bother you."

They turned and left. Mom and Dad waited silently by the door, listening to the officers' footsteps die away in the distance.

Dad closed the door. He grinned. "Well, Daniel, a parent's worst nightmare is the time his teenage son shows up late with the police as his escort. What has our wild and rebellious son done this time? Drugs, reckless driving, a drunken brawl?"

I sighed. Dad was teasing. I showed up hours late with the police, and he still trusted me. "I took pictures of the police station. It never occurred to me that that might seem like a breach of national security."

I gave them a quick rundown of my last several hours. "I guess I never should have taken a picture of a government building that deals with security. Actually I took lots of pictures of it. I suppose that looked suspicious. But it was the outside of a public building. What could be so dangerous about that?"

Dad suggested we download my pictures and see if I had accidentally photographed something that could threaten security.

I popped the memory card out of my camera and slipped it into the card reader. The clues were gone and the card was blank. Three weeks of pictures had disappeared.

I was relieved to be home, but irritated too. I had tried so hard to be careful in China, and I got interrogated for taking innocent pictures of a police building. Why couldn't they crack down on vegetable stall owners who overcharged and bicycle thieves instead?

I wanted to complain about my problems to someone, but I couldn't e-mail Melody about the police. I had to write as if each e-mail was monitored.

I wanted to tell Jason about my troubles. But I had already shown disrespect for his government by complaining about the One Child Policy. I still needed to put that right.

When I told Chuck what happened, he reminded me that I should have known better than to take lots of pictures of an area with high security.

"God protected you, Daniel," he said. "God knows you weren't trying to offend anyone. You weren't hurt, and you can take your pictures again. But God does expect us to learn from our mistakes."

Wasn't there another way to learn?

I couldn't change the fact my bike was stolen, so I tried to forget it. But as I walked around Huajiang, I couldn't help scanning every bikestand, searching for my shiny blue bike. All my hard-earned money had bought me a few weeks of bicycle.

I knew why people were unfair, but God confused me. Why did God allow unfairness? Mom always said God honors us when we put Him first. I had given my life to Him and left my youth group for my whole senior year. I had left my culture to adapt to a Chinese one. American culture formed a big chunk of my personality. I'd given up a chunk of *me* to reach out to Chinese people. What more did God want?

Days passed and it was time for my Bible study with Jason. We were studying the book of Daniel now. I still hadn't resolved things with God, but I didn't want to hurt Jason. So I stuffed my feelings inside, deciding to work on my problems later.

The doorbell buzzed, and I opened the door to a grinning Jason. He was always glad to see me, but this grin suggested Jason was hiding something.

I poured us glasses of Coke and set a plate of fragrant melon on the kitchen table.

"Daniel, I must tell you good news! On Sunday I dare to ask my parents if I may be baptized. They say I may!"

That explained the grin. "That's great, Jason. Were they OK with that? I mean, did they seem happy or at least—not mad?"

"They say it is my decision. I think when they see Li Huo is a Christian and she is kind, they think to be a Christian is not so bad. I am so happy. Now I can obey God and obey parents too. Thank you for praying for me."

I told him I was glad to do it.

He pulled a bright pink dragon fruit out of his backpack. "I bring dragon fruit to celebrate." Not that he ever came empty handed.

He cut the long green spikes off the fruit, peeled and sliced it. I had always wanted to try one of these. I nibbled a piece of the white insides. Sweet. The little black seeds reminded me of kiwi fruit but the taste was . . . how could I describe it? A surprise.

"Did you find your bicycle?" Jason asked.

"No." After Jason's good news, it didn't seem so important.

"It is sad. You come over ocean to China to teach me Bible, and this bad thing happens. God knows. He understands. Yes?"

"Yes." God knows and He allowed it to happen anyway. I was the one who didn't understand.

"It is like our Bible friend Daniel."

"What do you mean?"

"Daniel must go far from home to Babylon. He cannot do as he wants. He must leave home and parents. But Daniel know only one thing is important. He must serve God."

I bet no one in Babylon stole Daniel's bicycle. But I didn't say so. Still all this talk about the oppressive Babylonian government reminded me of some unfinished business.

"Yes. Daniel served the Lord. He served in the government too. He didn't have any choice about that, but he served well. He didn't always agree with the government, but he found a way to work with it. Daniel actually served three kings of two different countries. He lived for God his whole life while serving in high positions in governments that worshiped false gods."

"Wow. Daniel was great man."

"Daniel was incredible. When I study about him with you, I realize this. We can learn many things from Daniel. When you took me to visit your dorm room, I said that the government has no right to make the One Child Policy. I really criticized your government. I'm sorry, Jason. I shouldn't have said those things. Christians need to respect the government."

"It's OK, Daniel. It is difficult for you to live in China. I know this. But you are so good to me. You teach me Bible. You are good friend. Every day I thank God you come to China."

Thankfulness was great, but he didn't have to overdo it. It made me feel even more guilty.

"Daniel, I think everyday about William. You say, be careful, tell him about Jesus some day. When do you think we can tell William?"

"Not yet. It just doesn't seem like the right time to tell him."

"Why not right time? William needs to know about Jesus. Is it true?"

"Yes." I shrugged. "But I don't know when we ought to tell him."

Jason scribbled a sentence on my notebook. "Chinese have saying. 'If you don't go into the cave of the tiger, how are you going to get its cub?'"

"Where do you get this stuff?"

Jason shrugged. "I buy Chinese-English proverb book. If William does not believe on Jesus, he will die and go to hell like my grandfather. Is it true?"

"Yes."

"Tiger cave is dangerous, but one must go into cave to get tiger cub. If we do not tell William about Jesus, how can he believe?"

I forked a chunk of melon and stuck in my mouth, stalling for time. "I want to tell him. I do. I'm praying that God will show me the right time."

He nodded. "Chuck also say we must be careful. But it is very good news! Creator God know me, love me. Jesus die to forgive me. Of course I want to tell my friends."

"Jason, I'm glad you want to tell your friends about Jesus. But we need to do that . . ." How did Chuck put it? ". . . in a quiet way."

We turned to our Bible study then. Shadrach, Meshach, and Abednego didn't bow down to the idol when their government leader told them to. When strictly commanded to do something the Old Testament clearly forbade, they refused. I wondered how much they actually talked about God in that pagan society.

We finished our lesson and our fruit. I walked Jason to the door and said goodbye. He quickly stepped out of sight, but I listened as his footsteps echoed down each flight of stairs until the outside door slammed. I couldn't forget the way his eyes shone when he talked about God. "Creator God know me, love me. Jesus die to forgive sins." I had lost my wonder for that simple truth. A stolen bike was unfair, but compared to this truth, was it really important?

Meanwhile our Sunday Bible studies sparked with excitement. We had finally scheduled our first baptism for the last Sunday in October. Pastor Mark Chen, a Chinese pastor from another part of China, was flying in to perform the actual baptism. Twelve people had asked to be baptized. Pastor Mark would talk to them individually. If they could convince him they were truly saved and understood baptism, he would baptize them. This was our first baptism. When it was over, we could organize into a real house church.

The Sunday before, we took one last offering to cover Pastor Mark's expenses. Chuck had already bought the ticket, mainly with his own money, but he wanted to offer the Chinese one last opportunity to help.

Chuck told everyone about the small farm outside of town where we would have "our outing." Christians owned this farm on the edge of a forested area. All the leaves would be turning colors. We could bring lunches and enjoy our time together. While we were at it, we would use the little pond for our baptism.

Daisy dropped several coins into the Tupperware offering bowl. "I invite many friends to baptism. Is it OK?"

Chuck coughed but kept a straight face. "Who did you invite?"

Daisy smiled. "I invite three classmates and Hu Xiao. Hu Xiao English name is Rain. I talk to Hu Xiao on phone. He want to come too. Is it OK?"

Chuck rumpled his red hair. "Do you know these people well?"

"Three classmates I know long time. Hu Xiao before is my classmate. Now he work at newspaper. One day I think about baptism. Hu Xiao call, say 'Happy Birthday.' I think I must invite Hu Xiao to baptism."

An unsaved reporter—just what we needed at our secret baptism.

Chuck repeated his little invite-friends-carefully talk.

Jason told about his parents giving him permission to be baptized. Sunny said she would wait until the next baptism when she hoped her husband would come. Ken asked us to pray for him because he was afraid of water.

After the Bible study they left in groups until only our family remained. Susan had invited us for lunch so that they could discuss the baptism with my parents.

Over spaghetti we discussed the reporter Daisy had invited to the baptism. Had we taken every reasonable precaution to keep the baptism safe? What would we do if a dangerous person showed up?

In the end we had to leave it in God's hands, trusting Him to keep our group safe.

I told Chuck how Jason had asked if I had witnessed to William yet. "When are we supposed to be careful, and when are we supposed to be bold?"

Chuck sighed. "Susan and I have been here more than two years now, and that question is never far from our minds. If we say too much, we might get kicked out of China. If we say too little, no one will get saved. Some Ms are not as careful as we are, but we want to have a long and lasting ministry. So far we've seen about eighteen people get saved. They have studied with us long enough to get a good foundation of knowledge. They seem to have a clear understanding of salvation. Most of them made the decision on their own and only told us about it afterward. Some might say we should be bolder, but we believe that this approach is the way the Lord is leading us."

I frowned. I had heard all this before—more than once. It didn't help. I forked my spaghetti around the plate. "Do you ever wonder if we're being . . ."

"Paranoid?"

"Yeah."

"It does seem strange that many Chinese don't seem to be afraid to talk freely about these things. New Christians e-mail us or call us on the phone and ask us if the Bible study is at our house Sunday morning at ten." Chuck grinned. "The government must know about our meetings. Officials could save us a lot of trouble if they'd just put an ad in the paper, 'Bible study at Harveys' house every Sunday morning at ten.' Yet the authorities haven't stopped us."

"Maybe we don't need to be so careful. You said yourself that China is allowing more religious freedom now. If they know and they don't crack down on us, doesn't that make you think that we're OK?"

Chuck sighed. "When we meet Chinese who have been Christians for many years, they tell us to be careful. When we meet Christians who are Party members, they tell us to be careful too."

"You know Communists who are Christians?"

Chuck nodded. "You do too. Max belongs to the party."

"Max is a CP member? I-happened-to-be-reading-the-Song-of-Solomon Max? Max who's getting baptized in one week? That Max?"

"Yup. That Max. He was one of our first contacts in Huajiang. He studied with us over a year before he got saved. When we went back to the States for six months, he read the entire Bible. Now he's on the second time through."

"And he's been a Party member all that time?"

"Yup. He joined the Communist Youth League in high school, then the Communist Party when he turned eighteen. It's not easy to back out of the Party once you've joined. So he is a Party member and a very careful Christian. Max will never call on the phone and ask dangerous questions. Max will be careful who he invites to the baptism. Max doesn't say much, but he always reminds us to be careful."

If we thought our new believers were careless on the phone before, the week of the baptism was worse.

Sunny called Chuck and asked if it was too late for her to be baptized. Her husband was thinking about coming.

Ken called us to find out what bus to take to "the baptism."

Several others called for directions to "the outing" but ended up talking about the baptism.

Jason called me several times just to tell me he couldn't wait to be baptized.

A few called from their cell phones to ours, but most used landline phones which were easier to trace. So much for our secret baptism.

Saturday Dad picked Pastor Mark up from the airport. The Harveys came to our house to make plans over lunch. After everyone arrived, we'd sing a few songs, Pastor Mark would preach, and we'd have the baptism. Then we'd have time for lunch and fellowship walking around the farm. That afternoon we'd discuss our doctrinal statement and talk about the church organization.

After making plans for Sunday, Pastor Mark met with the ones who wanted to be baptized. He met with some at our house and some at the Harveys'. By bedtime Saturday night everything seemed to be in order. Everyone had directions to the farm. Mom had lunch prepared and waiting in the fridge. The plans were complete.

I had trouble sleeping that night. We had come to China to help the Harveys start a church. Tomorrow would be the beginning of that church.

I laid awake so long that Mom had to shake me awake the next morning. I downed a bowl of oatmeal. We gathered our stuff and headed for the bus.

Forty-five minutes on a crowded bus brought us a short walk from the farm. We met the Harveys and Pastor Mark on the way and walked in with them. Soon others arrived in little groups. We strolled around the farm, picked up fallen leaves, ate melon seeds.

Sunny showed up without her husband. She decided to be baptized anyway. Daisy scampered in with five friends. Max drove up in his car with Ken and Julie. I kept checking the road for any sign of Jason.

Mom sent me to tour the rice fields with several new people who had started coming. I guess she could tell I was getting antsy.

Finally everyone had arrived but Jason. Chuck said we ought to start singing. We sang "God is So Good" several times, and I checked the road once more. Jason was just rounding the corner, but who was with him?

No. Lord, please don't let it be . . . please, not—William!

Jason's grinned from ear to ear. "I brought my friend William."

I eyed Dad.

Dad coughed. "Well, William. We didn't know you were coming."

William smiled. "I see Li Jing waiting for a bus. I ask him where he is going. He say he is going to a baptism. I hear about Christian baptism. I always want to know 'what is baptism?'" William held up a camera. "Jason say I may come."

Jason glanced at Chuck. "It is OK if I invite William?"

Chuck's smile froze. "William's dad is Brett's boss at the university. Since William's dad works with Daniel's dad, William and Daniel have become friends. William has been showing Daniel around Huajiang. William is also is Jason's classmate. So, William, you decided to join our little outing today. It is very beautiful out here in the country, especially now that the leaves are changing colors. We brought lunches with us too. Will you be able to join us for lunch?"

"Sure. Jason say after baptism you will be here all day. I can stay for whole time."

Chuck glanced around the group. "Well, we have a song to teach you. Brett, you can help Daniel teach this one."

Dad had never been a great singer, but he read over the English words for "What a Friend We Have in Jesus." Then he and I sang the first verse. Chuck slipped over to Pastor Mark's chair and whispered to him. I could imagine a change in plans.

Pastor Mark preached next. It was the first sermon I ever heard in Chinese, and I was anxious to see how much I could understand. But two months of Chinese class didn't help me much. I caught a lot of the words, but missed much of the meaning. Now and then Jason leaned over my direction and gave a rough translation.

"Pastor Mark say, 'The Bible say God give government for our good. Christians should be good citizens. Christians should respect government. Christians should obey government whenever possible.'"

Funny message for a baptism. This went on for about five minutes.

"Pastor Mark say, 'Christians are baptize to obey God. Baptism is not'—how do you say it? 'Magical. Water does not change you. Does not save you. It is symbol.'"

This part was shorter. In fifteen minutes the whole sermon was done.

Sermon over, we headed for the pond. Clouds darkened the sky as Pastor Mark slipped off his shoes and socks and waded into the water. Gingerly he worked his way over mossy rocks. A duck landed on the water and floated over to see who was on his pond. Suddenly the bottom dropped off. Pastor Mark teetered on the uneven bottom, then worked to steady himself.

He caught Jason's eye. "Li Jing, would you like to go first?"

Jason waded out into the water. His foot slipped on a mossy rock. He glanced at me. "I fear water. Will you go with me?"

I slipped off my shoes and socks and waded out to Jason. I grabbed his arm to steady him. A camera flashed, and I noticed William grinning.

Jason's proverb popped into my mind. "If you don't go into the cave of the tiger, how are you going to get its cub?

The cool, dark water made me shiver. In my mind the friendly little pond had become a tiger's cave.

NINE

We survived the baptism and waited to see if anything terrible would happen. After that the last person I wanted to see was William, my personal Blabby Abby.

After the baptism my family decided I needed to be too busy to see William for awhile. I started some cleaning projects for Mom. We set some early deadlines for my school work. Our family took a couple of days off to do some sightseeing. But I couldn't put him off forever.

The next time I saw him, we kept busy playing computer games at a nearby internet bar. On the way home, however, William found his chance.

We got off the bus and walked under an underpass, known as a *fly-over* to the Chinese. Several shops were built under the fly-over. We stopped at one shop to buy some Chinese pastries.

William paid for them, then handed me one. "I do not understand Christian baptism. Why do Christians do this?"

I glanced left and right. The shopkeeper had gone into the back of the store. Traffic noise covered the sound of our voices. William's ears were the only ones I worried about—as if they weren't enough.

"In the Bible God tells Christians they should do this to show they are Christians."

"If they do this, they can go to Christian heaven?"

"Baptism doesn't help them get to heaven. It just shows they are Christians—kind of like a wedding ring. If I put a wedding ring on, it wouldn't make me married. But my dad wears a wedding ring so people will know he is married."

William bit into his pastry and licked the red bean paste that dribbled out. "Have you ever been baptized?"

"Yes. I was baptized when I was a kid in America."

"So who is Mark, the man who baptized people?"

"He lives somewhere else in China. I don't really know much about him."

We crossed a busy street. William led us down a side road. "I am curious. Why did your father not baptize Jason?"

"Why should he baptize Jason? He's just a math and English teacher."

"Did he baptize people in America?"

"No. Why would he do that?"

William shrugged. "I do not know about Christian things."

How could I put a good slant on this? "Christians like to meet other Christians. When we came to China, Jason wanted to have an American friend like you wanted an American friend. I found out he was a Christian. I was glad to meet a Christian my age in China. Since he is my friend, I wanted to see him get baptized. Jason also teaches me Chinese sayings and Chinese culture. I am very interested in Chinese music. Did I tell you about the time Jason took me to a music store and the owner taught me how to play the pipa?"

I quickened my pace. By the time I finished talking about music we had reached our apartment. I gave William an over-eager goodbye.

I climbed the stairs to our apartment with a prayer on my lips. "Thank you, Lord. I didn't end up telling William anything he didn't already know."

The official Party line was that China had no house churches. Party officials admitted that there were occasional Bible studies for weak or elderly people who couldn't make it to the Three Self Patriotic Church. And once in a while Christians might get to-gether between their regular meetings at the Three Self Church. But why would China need house churches? People could be Christians and could freely go to the public, state approved, Three Self Church.

"Lord, could you just keep William from asking about the C-word and the M-word?" I prayed. "And please keep me from saying anything that could endanger Jason or any other Chinese believer."

Thanksgiving landed on a day when Dad and Chuck had to teach. We ate a Pizza Hut pizza at the Harveys' house. Would Christmas be any better?

I woke up December first and flipped my calendar. I checked the view from my bedroom window. Dusty pathways and well-worn grass wound their way between the columns of apartment buildings. Sigh. I was wearing four layers of clothing trying to stay warm inside our apartment, but there would be no snow this Christmas.

"Adventure or oatmeal?" I mumbled. The stairs took longer than usual that morning. I trudged my way to the breakfast shop and hunted for something special, anything special, to lift my spirits. By now we had tried everything on the menu. I ordered some steamed bread with dipping sauce and the Chinese omelet. On the way home I chose one Christmas red apple from the fruit stand.

Our family gathered for breakfast. We thanked the Lord for the food. I pulled the food from the bags and plunked the apple in the middle of the table. "Merry Christmas. This red apple is our first official Christmas decoration because today is the first day of December. So what are we going to do for Christmas?"

Dad checked the calendar. "December already? Where does the time go?"

I rolled my eyes.

Mom dished out the omelet. "Don't worry, Daniel. We haven't forgotten about Christmas. Dad's been looking for a Christmas tree. And I've been thinking about asking the Harveys to spend Christmas Day with us."

Dad poured the bag of dipping sauce into a bowl. "Christmas will be a little different this year, but remember, we're actually living in China! A few years ago we never would have imagined we'd be doing that. Maybe the holiday will give us special opportunities to witness. Susan's planning a Christmas party for our church." Dad whispered the last word. We whispered the C-word in our home. It reminded us to be careful about using it.

I tried to smile, but it didn't sound much like Christmas. After several hours of homeschool, I wandered through a few stores but couldn't find any Christmas presents.

That night Dad called from the street on his cell phone. "Daniel, I'm just getting out of a pedicab with our Christmas tree. You want to come help me?"

I took the stairs two at a time. Dad waited by the street beside a big pot with a scrawny tree in it.

"That's a Christmas tree?"

"It's a Norfolk Pine. It's a little different from the pine trees in Washington, but at least it's not one of those cheap, imitation trees."

I thought a cheap imitation tree might look better than this one, but I didn't say so.

Dad and I tried carrying the pot together. That was awkward. After trying several positions he lugged it up one flight of steps, and I lugged it up the next.

Mom waited at the top of the stairs. She had cleared a spot for the tree on the table by the window.

Dad hefted the tree to the tabletop.

Mom stepped back and sized up the tree. "It'll grow on us. We can use that tree for years to come."

While Dad had been out searching for a Christmas tree, Mom had bought a box of twelve small Christmas bulbs. We each chose four different colored bulbs—red, green, blue, and gold—and hung them on the tree.

Mom stood back and examined it with her decorator's eye. "It still needs something."

I told her I'd fix it. I cut out a cardboard star and covered it with aluminum foil. With a rubber band I attached the star to the top of the tree.

Mom smiled unevenly. "Well, Merry Christmas."

"Yeah." Pathetic, pitiful. This was a Christmas tree? "Wait till Melody hears we have a real tree. Her family always goes artificial."

I wrote Melody that night.

Dear Melody,

It's December first, and I saw my first store Christmas decorations today. The big department store near us had a few tinsel ornaments hanging around and a rack of ornaments and Christmas cards. I guess it's amazing they celebrate Christmas at all considering its origins.

We got our Christmas tree. It's a real one, but it's in a pot and looks more like a large house plant than a Christmas tree. It's going to be a weird Christmas. I guess a little snow would help.

Don't get me wrong. I'm glad we're here. But think of us this Christmas. It's kind of a letdown compared to our usual holiday.

Merry Christmas,
Daniel

I knew that Christ's birth was the really important part about Christmas. Everything else, the presents and decorations and parties, were just the wrapping paper around this great Gift. But I missed the wrapping paper. And if I missed that stuff, Mom and Dad would too.

In the States Mom decorated every room in the house and then started on the church building. She spent days cutting Christmas cookies into shapes, baking them, and decorating them. Last year she made a whole gingerbread village. But now all her decorating stuff was crammed into boxes in our basement in Seattle.

What could I do to make Christmas special for our family? I would have to hunt hard to find nice gifts for Mom and Dad. And I couldn't forget Jesus. It was His birthday, after all. For the last several years I had tried to think of one thing I could do for others as a gift to Him. Last year I had helped an eighty-four-year-old lady clean out her garage. The year before that I baby-sat, free, for a single mom. What could I do in China?

While I tried to think of ideas, I got an e-mail back from Melody.

Dear Daniel,

I made you something. It's not big and exciting, but I hope it will help you not to be homesick for Christmas. I am sending it by snail mail.

Just remember—our Best Friend was away from home for His first Christmas too.

Thinking of you and your family,
Melody.

Our Best Friend, Jesus, was away from home for His first Christmas. Our pastor in Seattle called it "His stepping down." Jesus stepped down from the unimaginable glories of heaven to become the baby in a poor Jewish family. What was that like for Him?

I decided to walk around the shops in our area and think about that. Mom and Dad were gone, so I scrawled a note to say where I was going and clumped down the stairs.

I passed overflowing garbage dumpsters and littered sidewalks. On the main street an old man blew his nose, hard, forcing the slimy stuff to drop on the sidewalk. That didn't happen in America. But then, I don't suppose the angels blew their noses on the golden streets of heaven either. Was it hard for Jesus to get used to living on earth?

I strolled past a glitzy department store and entered a back alley. A barefoot toddler played on the filthy street beside his mother. She called to me to buy the vegetables that she had spread on a tarp on the ground. The sun hung high in the sky, but a side of pork dangled from one stall beside the skin from the pig's head.

I usually blocked this part of China from my mind, but even in this modern bustling city, it was a real part.

Chuck had started this English ministry because of his limitations in Chinese. We reached out to one tiny segment of Chinese society, the part we were most comfortable with. But nine million people crowded into Huajiang. The things that made me pull back and look away were everyday reality for many. My American culture made some Chinese things seem disgusting and rude. And I supposed that some American ways seem disgusting and rude to the Chinese.

I couldn't imagine the angels being anything other than well-behaved and refined. They worshiped Jesus. Did He find earth's manners to be disgusting and rude?

I ambled past a fruit stand where a Chinese baby lay in an infant seat. The mother dangled a string above his head. The little hand groped for the string, reaching out with jerky movements, missing and trying again.

I imagined Jesus in Bethlehem, reaching out for the first time to grasp some dangling object. Almighty God trapped in an uncoordinated body. God incognito. Yes, His first Christmas must have been a rude awakening too.

I wandered out of the open air market and roamed down the side streets of our area. I searched for all the negative sights of Huajiang, the things I habitually ignored.

A ragged little boy pointed to me and called out to his grandfather. I could understand his Chinese now. He was laughing at my huge American nose and my white skin. I squatted down and spoke to him in Chinese. He disappeared behind his grandfather's legs. Sometimes Jesus must have felt like a foreigner too.

After about an hour I passed a bike rack. Habit made me scan the bikes for my shiny blue one. Some idiot had been riding *my* bike around Huajiang for two months!

Two months and it was still bugging me. I had worked hard for that bike. I had even locked it. But that shiny blue bike attracted a thief with a strong set of metal cutters. I was angry at the thief, and I was angry at God for letting it happen. But stolen bikes were part of living in China. Chuck said you weren't a missionary until you had your bike stolen.

Did the boy Jesus ever have his bike stolen? OK, Jesus didn't have a bike, but He would have owned some special toy. If someone stole His treasure, He could have exercised His omniscience to know who stole it. He could have zapped the thief with lightning. But I felt sure He didn't waste his omnipotence defending Himself and His property. Things just weren't that important—to Him. I, on the other hand, couldn't forget the injustice of a stolen bicycle. Maybe it was time I did.

I leaned on the bike rack and gave Jesus His Christmas present.

"Lord, the bike is Yours," I prayed. "If You want some thief to have it, that's up to You. I'm done worrying about it. You've asked me to live in China, and if that means losing my bike, that's a small price to pay for following You."

I turned away from the bikes and walked home. On the way I passed the lady who used to overcharge me for vegetables. I watched while a taxi nearly ran into a motor scooter.

Jesus chose to live in an unfair world. I needed Him to teach me how to do the same.

A week later, while I was still meditating on Christmas, William called. He said he needed help with an English speech. Could he come to my house? We scheduled a time.

Before he arrived, I looked up "Christmas" on the internet. I found the Christmas story in its basic form. I printed it out and read it over until I had practically memorized it. I could say any of these things to William, and it would be no more than he could get off the internet by himself. That should be safe.

William came to our door with a bag of strawberries, which were hugely expensive this time of year. "Thank you for helping me, Daniel. This speech is very important. My teacher choose me to represent university in speech contest. I am honored she choose me, but I feel much pressure to succeed."

I told him I was glad to help.

"I choose speech topic as American holiday of Christmas because I have American friend to help me. I think you can help me be number one person."

I set the berries on the coffee table and invited William to sit down. "So what do you want to know?"

"How do Americans celebrate Christmas?"

I showed him our pitiful little Christmas tree.

He lifted a white cutout that hung on a branch. "Before I see Christmas trees. But this? Never. What is this?"

I smiled. "Those are snowflakes. Remember my friend Melody? She made them for us. She knew I would miss the snow in Seattle, so she sent me fake snow. She cut ten different designs, because no two snowflakes are alike."

"What is Christmas about snow?"

"Well, in America, in many places, it snows at Christmastime. And snow reminds us of Santa Claus, which is a Christmas story."

"I know about Santa Claus. I want to know the other Christmas story."

I was ready for this. I carried the strawberries to the kitchen to avoid eye contact. "Christmas is the time Christians celebrate the birth of Jesus Christ. Jesus is God's Son. Jesus was born to a poor family. He died thirty-three years later. Christians believe Jesus became alive again. They believe He now lives with His Father in heaven."

"That is all?"

"Well, that's the basic story."

"Why do Christians believe this is so important?"

"Well, Christians believe Jesus came to make peace between God and men. You know how Chinese have matchmakers and mediators? Like when business people have a problem. They hire someone else to go back and forth between them and work it out."

William nodded.

"Well, Jesus was kind of like that. He worked out the problems between God and people."

"Now, no more problem?"

I sat across the table from William. How much should I say? "Actually, if you want to know about this, you could read the Bible. Everything Christians believe comes from the Bible. You could go buy a Bible at the Three Self bookstore."

William nodded. "OK. I think I must have a quote of you for my essay. What do you think is best part of Christmas?"

I scratched my head. "Well, there are many good things about Christmas, but one really fun part is that you get to do fun things with your family."

"But most of your family is not in China."

Good point. "You're right, but I can still do fun things with my parents and my Chinese friends."

That seemed to satisfy William. He scribbled my words in his notebook. "You are good friend, Daniel, to help me do speech. This speech cause me big problem."

"Why is that?"

"Usually I get speeches and essays off internet. This teacher is very strict. He checks internet."

"You mean, you copy your essays off the internet?"

"Why not? Every student in China does this."

"But that's—cheating. I mean, the whole point of going to school is to learn things. How can you learn if you copy someone else's paper?"

William shrugged. "One must learn how to find good information. Finding information. Thinking of information. It is the same value."

I frowned. "I don't think your teachers would agree with that."

"Teachers are not stupid. They know students do not think of everything without help. Perhaps you do not do this in America. In China, no problem."

How could you answer that? I was speechless.

"Daniel, you have your God to help you. Is it true?"

"Yeah."

"I am my own god. I can conquer difficulties by myself. I must make my future secure. I will do what I must do to make it work."

"Even if that means cheating? Doesn't it matter if something is right or wrong? Where will you stop? Would you do anything to succeed?"

William shook his head. "I think Americans are very strange. You talk about right and wrong. Who can say what is right and wrong? You talk about believing. In China, action is more important than believing. Family is more important than feeling. My parents once very poor. They work very hard. During hard times in China they obey leaders, do not cause trouble. Today my parents provide good life for me. I must provide good life for them when old. I must provide good life for my child one day. I must not be weak link in chain. I must make my future secure."

I wondered how far William would go to make his future secure. Would he turn in a friend for going to an unregistered church or recruiting new believers?

TEN

"Weird" and "ugly" usually weren't Christmas adjectives, but this wasn't going to be the usual Christmas.

As we got closer to Christmas, I lowered my expectations of the holiday. This year would be different. We wouldn't have a big Christmas church service. Turkey or ham was out of the question. And the presents would probably be, like I said, a little weird. I had a hard time finding a good gift for Mom and Dad, so they would probably have a hard time finding one for me.

But Chuck and Susan made me curious. They had already bought me a present, but Chuck kept dropping hints that it was unconventional, humble, then ugly. "I hope you like it," he said. "It could come in handy, but it might not look like much at first."

Nothing good could follow those words, right? But Chuck and Susan were always good to me. They treated me more like a co-worker than a kid. I told myself to expect disappointment, but the curiosity drove me crazy. What could it be?

On Christmas morning Chuck and Susan were supposed to arrive at our house about ten. I watched the clock flip over to 10:08 before a commotion broke out in the stair well. Dad opened the door, but he wouldn't let me peek. "Need some help down there?" he called.

Susan giggled. "We'll make it."

After several minutes of huffing and puffing and bumping and banging, Susan backed into view. With her came the ugliest bike I've ever seen, with a red ribbon tied to the handlebars. Susan must have spotted the skepticism in my eyes.

"Merry Christmas, Daniel. Chuck has had a lot of fun fixing this bike up for you. This is actually a very good bike in disguise."

And a good disguise it was.

"Chuck bought this bike from an old sock peddler." Susan shook the metal rack that was welded onto the back. "The man carried his socks in a big plastic bin on this rack and he drove all over our part of Huajiang selling socks. He owned this bike for eighteen years. It was made sturdy for deliverymen. It's rusty, but sound and very sturdy."

Somehow sturdy and cool didn't come together yet in my mind.

Chuck squeezed the fat tires. "The tires are new, but I used the original rims so the bike would—match."

The tires were pretty dirty for being new. "Did you ride it from your house?"

Chuck grinned. "We brought it in a taxi. I had to work hard to get the tires that dirty."

"I get it. You wanted them to—match."

"You're catching on. I oiled the bell and bought new handle grips. So what you have is a very sturdy, dependable bike that no one will steal."

I had a choice. I could laugh or cry. I chose to laugh. "This is the weirdest Christmas present I have ever gotten, but you're right. It is a very dependable bike that no one will steal. Thank you for all the work you put into it."

"If you wear a hat and dark glasses, you might pass for an old sock peddler," Chuck teased. "If we need to spy out anything, you're our man."

"Incognito," I muttered.

"What's that?"

"Never mind."

Jesus stepped down from heaven to become our Savior. And this bike was a definite step down from the shiny blue bike I had bought. Jesus had His reasons for coming to earth as a humble servant. And God had His reasons for giving me a bike fit for an old sock peddler. I wanted to be like Jesus, but I had never expected it to be like this. Who said God didn't have a sense of humor?

We played games and shared silly jokes with Chuck and Susan.

For dinner Chuck and Dad and I walked to KFC for a bucket of fried chicken. Mom whipped up real mashed potatoes, and Susan made gravy from chicken broth she had brought along. We ate cheese sauce on our broccoli and put ice in our Coke. Mom made a homemade cheesecake from ingredients she bought at a shop that sold foreign goods. For this one day we could relax, eat American food, tell American jokes, and not feel guilty about it. Tomorrow we would go back to trying to fit into Chinese culture again.

After dinner Mom stacked the leftovers in the fridge, and we sat around a table filled with dirty dishes.

Dad fingered his napkin. Colonel Sanders' head hovered above the Chinese characters for Kentucky Fried Chicken. "Well, our family has made huge changes in the last five months. I've learned a lot, yet I've never realized so clearly how little I know, and how much I have to learn. Coming here has changed me. Since it's Christmas, I'd like to have everyone name one thing that they like about China."

Chuck spoke first. "I like how our Chinese believers get excited when they learn something new from the Bible. And I'm glad for good public transportation so I don't have to drive in the busy traffic."

"I like the food," Susan said. "All the different kinds of greens they have at the market and the loquats and dragonfruit. I really like the moon cakes our bakery makes for Mid-Autumn Festival. And I'm really thankful for all the cheap little restaurants around our house."

Dad said he was glad that all the exercise he got climbing stairs had put him in good shape.

Mom talked about her Bible studies with Fiona and finding out she had decided to become a Christian. "I like the fresh soybeans too," she said. "They really make a nice stir-fry with chicken. They're good for you, and easy to make. I hope they're still selling them in our store in America when we go back."

Everyone looked at me. "I'm glad I could learn about Chinese music and play the pipa."

Dad raised his eyebrows. "Is that it?"

"Well this Christmas I've been thinking about how Jesus stepped down from heaven to earth. Living in China has made me realize a tiny bit of the huge changes He made when He did that. He didn't just get busy and die for our sins and go back to heaven. He lived here thirty-three years and felt what it was like to be a baby, then a child, and grow to be a man. Hebrews says living on earth helped Him to understand our weaknesses. He goes between us and God the Father and brings us grace and mercy when we need it. Jesus knew what it was like to live in a place where people had very different ideas about what was important and right. So I guess He understands if I get confused."

"Living in a foreign country can be confusing." Chuck rumpled his thick, curly hair. "There's nothing like being a tall redhead in China to remind you that you don't fit in. But it does give you a different perspective on life."

"It sure does." I scribbled on my napkin, coloring Colonel Sanders' hair black. "I have lots to learn about Chinese culture, but I hope in the next six months I can begin to see things more from a Chinese perspective."

Chuck punched my arm. "You've got a good start, Daniel. We can see you growing in many ways. You're a good addition to our ministry team."

I smiled. "Oh. I almost forgot another thing about China. I like those chewy little sesame balls too."

Christmas Day lifted my spirits but the next day we got a reality check.

Since all of the students in our Chinese class were foreigners, we got Christmas Day off. The next day, however, we were back in class.

During break Brittany searched for a moment when I was standing by myself. She gazed out the window, smiling, as if discussing the weather. "Daniel, I need to talk to you."

"OK."

"After class meet me at the stationery store down the road."

During the next hour I could hardly concentrate wondering what Brittany wanted. After class I walked with Adam to the university gate. Then we separated, and I ambled down the street to the store.

Brittany was admiring some pencil cases in the window. "Well, hello, Daniel," she said, as if our meeting was entirely accidental. She glanced around to see that no one was watching us. "I'd like to go home with you for a few minutes if you don't mind."

I agreed. We sauntered off toward our apartment. Once in the door her attitude changed from friendly banter to strictly business. I called Mom and Dad over and offered Brittany a seat. She chose to stand.

"I know you are friends of Chuck's," she said. "My co-workers know a little bit about him. Though we may have our doctrinal differences, we know you are involved with a house church like we are. My co-workers asked me to warn you.

"We meet every Sunday at the home of a Chinese believer. My co-workers and I normally go to every service, but last Sunday my school scheduled me to teach a make-up class so I couldn't go. My co-workers were both sick. They asked a Chinese believer to lead the service.

"We meet at that same apartment every Sunday. Someone must have suspected we were a church. We haven't had any trouble before, but they were singing Christmas carols and apparently a neighbor complained about the noise. Some men from the Public Security Bureau showed up at the door."

"Was anyone arrested?"

"No. The Lord really protected us. They only asked two questions: 'Are there any foreigners here?' and 'Do you charge a membership fee?' Thankfully, they were able to answer 'no' to both questions."

Dad's knuckles had gone white. He relaxed his fists. "Whew. That was close."

"It sure was. Normally my co-workers and I would have been there. Now we know they are watching us. We think we need to make some changes."

"What kind of changes?"

"We need to find a new meeting place. We're also wondering about meeting on Saturday instead of Sunday. Any group which meets every Sunday is bound to look suspicious. And having us foreigners attached to it really draws attention to the group. We're not sure about all the changes we'll make, but we wanted to warn you to be more careful."

Mom put her hand on Brittany's shoulder. "Thank you. We'll talk to Chuck and Susan about it. Can I get you something to drink?" Mom must have noticed that Brittany looked a little wobbly.

Brittany shook her head. "Thanks, but I'd better go. You never know who could be watching my co-workers and me, so you might not want to be seen with us." She smiled weakly. "But we wanted to warn you, and since Daniel is in my Chinese class, they asked me to do it."

Brittany scurried down the stairs, and we stood staring at each other, trying to process this new news. We had come to China to lead Chinese to Christ and start a Chinese church. But since we were foreigners, our very presence endangered the group. Our white skin and big noses attracted attention to something which needed to remain incognito.

ELEVEN

"Maybe we should just go home. You know, back to America,"
I told Chuck. Our family was at the Harveys' home discussing
Brittany's news. "Brittany said the PSB asked if there were any
foreigners in the group. We're foreigners, and we attract attention
to our own group. Wouldn't it be safer for Chinese believers if all
the foreigners left? Now that we've started a church, maybe the
Chinese believers could get along without us."

Chuck sighed. "They could. They might not have the stamina
to keep the church going on its own, but they might. If they did,
what kind of church would they have? Max has been with us as
long as anyone. He asked me the other day if it is important to
believe that the Bible is all of God's revelation. He had heard there
were other books that were just as important as the Bible."

"Like what? The Book of Mormon?"

"Could be. Or he might be thinking of the Eastern Lightning
Movement. They believe that Jesus has come back to earth as a

Chinese woman. This new Jesus has written a third testament and plans to destroy the earth. Along with these Chinese cults we have all kinds of American false doctrine that is being taught. I don't know about you, Daniel, but I didn't come to China to get a few people saved and leave. I want to teach them sound doctrine and leave them with a church that will continue that teaching. When we have Chinese leaders who are trained to carry on this ministry I'll be happy to leave it in their hands. But we're not there yet. We've only begun."

I knew all that, but we had come to help Chinese people, and it just didn't seem right that we were putting them in danger. What could we do to make our little house church safer?

We needed to find another meeting place so we wouldn't have to meet in the same place all of the time. A group of Chinese gathering at the foreigners' house every Sunday morning had to look suspicious. Finding another place wouldn't be easy. Chuck and Susan had chosen to rent their particular apartment because it had a living room large enough for about twenty people. It was also a central location for our believers.

Maybe we could consider meeting on another day of the week. The early church met on Sunday because that was the day Jesus rose from the dead. So was it important for a church to meet on Sunday or would another day work as well? What did we have to do to remain biblical?

We discussed this for over an hour without reaching any definite conclusions. In the end we decided to pray about it, and we went home.

As we walked into our apartment, I picked up my guitar and started playing chord progressions. G, E minor, A minor, D, G. I strummed them over and over again, faster and faster, until they formed a sort of wild musical string.

Dad broke into my frenzy. "We're going to be all right, Daniel."

"How do you know?"

"Well, look at Brittany's group. God really protected them. The PSB came on the one night the foreigners weren't there. They didn't ask many questions, nothing that those believers couldn't answer honestly. And they've been warned. Now they know they need to change some things. We do too. Their little interview with the PSB has helped all of us."

"But it might not happen like that next time."

"It might not. But one thing will always be the same."

"What's that?"

"God will always be in control. We've been here more than four months. We've made some mistakes. Our Chinese friends call on the phone and say way too much. Yet we haven't gotten into trouble with the authorities so far."

"No. But that doesn't mean we won't."

"No, it doesn't. We knew there would be risks involved when we came here, but we came anyway because we have an important job to do. That hasn't changed. We need to continue to be careful, but God brought us to do a job, and I believe He's going to help us get that job done."

I set my guitar down. "Dad, do you ever feel like you just want to go home—to America?"

"Now and then."

"But you don't."

"When I feel like that, I have a Bible study with Ken and see how eager he is to learn. Or Sunny brings an unsaved friend to our Bible study who thinks she is so lucky to learn about the Bible. Or Max asks a really good question that shows he is growing. After that I don't want to go home anymore."

"I know what you mean. Jason gets so excited when he learns new stuff about the Bible. I know it's not like that on some other mission fields. He keeps wanting to witness to William, and I tell him to shut up. Am I being too careful?"

Dad scratched his head and smoothed the hair over his bald spot. "With William, I don't think so. Chuck has a funny feeling about him. His parents are CP members, and you tell us they're already pushing William to join the Party."

"But Communists need the Lord too, don't they?"

"Of course. But we also have to think about the safety of our group. William keeps asking detailed, personal questions. He knows a lot about us and Jason for someone who might want to impress the Party someday."

"So when am I supposed to witness to him? Never?"

"You have already told William several things about the Bible. See how he responds to that. Remember he came to Jason's baptism. Pastor Mark didn't end up saying anything about our church because William was there, but he presented the gospel clearly. I'm not saying you shouldn't say anything, but take it slow."

For several days I couldn't stop thinking about the PSB, but I couldn't stop thinking about William either.

"Lord, work in William's heart," I prayed. "I know I have to go slow with him, but he's the only unsaved Chinese person I know very well. He's my friend. He needs You, and I need to know You can use me. If You will allow me to lead William to salvation, I'll know You want me to be a missionary. That's not too much to ask for living in China ten months, is it?"

Thinking about Brittany's news and worrying about William wouldn't help anything. I needed to concentrate on something else. I still had lots to learn about China. I had already learned to pedal my rusty bike all over this part of Huajiang and ride buses and pedicabs and taxis. I could find most of the stuff our family needed to buy. I could speak a little Chinese and had grown to like a lot of Chinese foods. I had Chinese friends. I might have more to learn, but I was no tourist either.

Yet for all the facts I knew about China I seemed to be missing something. When I was with Jason and William, I understood most of what they said, but I didn't always follow their logic. During my last five months I needed to learn more about how Chinese think.

"Lord, help me to use the rest of my time in China well." I prayed. "Help me to be brave and careful at the same time. And help me to gain a deeper understanding of China so I can understand my Chinese friends better."

It sounded like a good prayer at the time, but I had no idea what I was praying for.

Jason finished his first semester at school and was preparing to go to his home in the country for the Chinese New Year's holiday. The Sunday before New Year's he came to our house church grinning.

"Daniel, I know good way for you to learn of Chinese New Year," he said. "Come to my home in Zhushan for three weeks New Year holiday in country."

I blinked. I wanted a deeper understanding of China, but three weeks of living with a Chinese family? "Well, Jason, it's really nice of you to ask me, but I don't want to interfere with your family time."

"It is no problem. I call my parents. They say it is good you come to our house. They want to meet my American friend. You can tell my parents about Bible. I think you must come."

Help, Lord, I prayed silently. *Am I getting in over my head with this?*

"There are beautiful mountains near my home. I think you must leave city, see another part of China."

"Well, Jason, it sounds really nice. I'll have to check with my parents first."

Jason's smile faded. "Maybe you do not want to stay at my home. It is very simple, not like American homes."

"Oh, no, Jason. I'm sure your home is very nice. You live there, so it must be fine. And I really would like to meet your parents."

"Then you must come."

I could tell my parents had broken off their conversations and were tuning into ours. "Uh, Dad, Jason would like me to go home with him for Chinese New Year's. I don't know if you have some special stuff planned for our family at that time."

Dad tried to read my face. I gave him a wobbly smile and raised my eyebrows.

He turned to Jason. "Well, Jason, that's really nice of you to invite Daniel. If Daniel wants to go home with you, that should be fine."

Mom cleared her throat. "Yes, but I think he'd better only stay for one week. After that I need Daniel's help at home."

I could have hugged her. One week of this adventure was good, but it was also enough. "Sure, Mom. That'll be OK. I can see a lot in a week. I can travel with Jason to his home and travel back on my own."

Jason pulled two tickets from his backpack. "We leave on train tomorrow, two o'clock."

"You already bought tickets? How did you know I would go?"

Jason grinned. "Like Chuck say, I have faith."

I had one day to pack my bags and prepare myself for my giant leap into Chinese culture. How hard could it be? I didn't know Jason's family, but he would be with me to translate and help me know what to do.

The next afternoon I rode a bus to the train station. On the bus I barely had room to stand, but the train station was worse. I had never seen so many people in one place. Most of China seemed to be traveling for the holidays.

I jumped onto a concrete planter and searched for Jason. How would I find him in this giant sea of Chinese heads? Finally a neon green notebook caught my eye. Jason was waving it. I pushed through the crowd to him, and we wiggled our way to the gate for our train.

Inside the train we were forced to stand for the duration. Jason said seat tickets were sold out when he bought them. The last passengers shoved past the doors as they squealed shut.

A man near Jason held a portable TV in his lap. A lady wearing a pink print shirt and orange print skirt set a live chicken at my feet. Its head poked out of a straw bag and pecked at my shoelaces.

Then the vendors squeezed by. Did I want to buy a magazine, gum, socks, or a little packet of toilet paper?

A man in a suit and tie leaned against the sign at the back of the car. "No spiting, no littering through windows, no smoking," the English translation read. I smiled. So were they really concerned about spitefulness or was it spitting they had in mind? The man searched his pockets, produced a match and some cigarettes and lit up.

Jason had joined a noisy discussion. I couldn't understand everything, but it was obvious that they were discussing me. Where was I from? Why was my nose so big? Were all Americans as fat as I was? How did Jason know me? How much did I pay for my name-brand sports shoes?

I set my backpack on my feet.

Jason told them that I could speak Chinese. That really made me a curiosity.

The lady with the chicken shouted at me, as if volume would help me understand her English. "How long you come China? You like China? China very good."

I tried to lower the volume as I answered her questions in my simple Chinese.

A well-dressed student snapped my picture with his cell phone.

A girl in a school uniform giggled. "You very tall. You play basketball like NBA?"

An old man beside Jason nudged him, asking him to translate. "He wants to know if Americans really own guns? He says in movies Americans shoot people. Is America very dangerous?"

The train lurched to a stop and another crowd of people pushed down the aisle. Did anyone ever get off the train or was everyone going to the country at Chinese New Year's?

Another vendor squeezed through the aisles offering bowls of hot noodles. I held up my bag with the sandwich. Several people, including Jason, bought noodles, and the rest wanted to investigate my lunch. I pulled out my sandwich, pulled the bread apart, and displayed the peanut butter and jelly. Jason, who was familiar with our family's diet, had to explain what it was.

A well-dressed lady squeezed through with a laptop computer strapped to her neck. Did anyone want to rent a computer and watch a movie? People shook their heads. Who needed movies when they had this interesting American to entertain them?

Every five minutes or so the train lurched to a stop. With each stop another crowd stepped on, forcing us to pack the aisles.

People finished their lunches. Some stuffed their garbage under their seats, and one man threw his out the window. The couple next to Jason played cards. Most dozed in an upright position, a Chinese talent I often wished I had.

After an hour Jason and I pushed through the crowd and barely made it out the doors before they closed. The train clacked away, leaving us in a small crowd of people who called Zhushan home. We stepped off the platform of the ancient train station. Small mountains formed a jagged skyline. Neat green plants trimmed the mountain side. So this was the country.

"Your village has nice mountains," I told Jason. "What is that growing on the side of them?"

"Bamboo. Zhushan means 'Bamboo Mountain.' But today mountains also grow tea. Many Zhushan people pick tea for their job."

I filled my lungs with country air. The smell of rancid garbage made me cough. OK. They had to pile their garbage somewhere. I'd get my breath of fresh air later.

As I glanced around I noticed that the countryside here was far different from the Idaho potato fields I must have been expecting. You could see a few rice fields and the occasional clump of bamboo. Huajiang's skyscrapers were missing. But this was no tiny village. Weathered red brick houses and concrete buildings stretched out as far as I could see. Some buildings rose five stories high.

We started down the road which formed the main street in Zhushan. Drab storefronts bordered the road.

Within five or ten blocks we passed the "business district." Grey housing blocks clustered around tiny dirt courtyards. Traditional red paper strips hung around the doorways making the only bright spots in the faded surroundings. Chinese characters ran along each strip. The paper was fresh only because the year was new.

Jason must have read the disappointment on my face. "Life in the country is very simple."

I nodded. I tried to think of a positive remark to make about the scene before me, but nothing came to mind.

We walked about a mile through the bedraggled village.

We had left the world of fashion behind. My friends in Huajiang definitely had a different sense of fashion from the States. Their wardrobes were limited, but their clothes were neater and dressier than the average American wore. The clothing of these villagers, however, were a definite step down from Huajiang.

Jason led me to a grey, two-story building with rows of mustard-colored doors. "My family lives on the second floor," he said.

We climbed the stairs, avoiding the broken stair rail which threatened to fall down. I missed the lights in our stairwells in Huajiang that came on when you clapped your hands. I had trouble seeing where I was going here. At the top we walked to the farthest two doors which belonged to Jason's home. He opened one door, slipped out of his shoes, and led me into a tiny living room with a TV and refrigerator.

His grandmother and father rose from cushionless wood furniture to meet us. His mother heard the commotion and left the small kitchen.

Jason's eyes shone as he introduced me in Chinese to his family.

His father smiled and nodded. "Daniel, very good meet Li Jing's American friend. Very happy you teach Li Jing English. You good English teacher."

"Jason has been a good friend to me too. He has helped me to learn many things about China." I grinned. "I don't know which one of us is the student and which one is the teacher. I guess we both are both things."

Mr. Li smiled and nodded again. "Sorry. My English very poor. Please to say again."

Keep it simple, Daniel. "Jason is my good friend."

Jason's father taught school in this village. If his English was any indication of the level of English spoken here, my limited Chinese would get lots of practice.

Mrs. Li brought us some warm 7-Up and some melon seeds. Jason led me through one of two small bedrooms to the restroom. The tiny, white-tiled room had only two objects—a Chinese toilet, which was little more than a ceramic hole in the floor, and a shower head.

I had now seen the whole house.

Jason, Mr. Li and I tried to make conversation over a TV program. Grandma and Mrs. Li chopped vegetables in the kitchen. The longer I sat, the colder I got. I could see my breath inside their house. My head started throbbing again, and I longed for a nap, but soon Jason's relatives started to arrive.

Four uncles and an aunt came, each with one child. One uncle was a policeman. Another uncle and Jason's only aunt were living hundreds of miles from their spouses, who weren't able to join us.

When the last one arrived, I leaned over to Jason. "I thought Chinese were supposed to have small families, like only one child."

"Now it is so. When my father was small child, this is not true. Government say must have large family to farm countryside. Then, too many people. Now must have only one child."

With each new group the noise level rose. Jason introduced me to each person, but even simple Chinese, with their country accent, was hard to understand. I soon became little more than a seat warmer. Far from offended, I was glad not to have to hold up my side of the conversation. It had been a long day.

I looked forward to dinner if only to relieve the boredom. Jiaozi, little pork dumplings that our family often ate, were traditional for New Year's. Good. Something familiar.

Everyone but the three on the wooden sofa sat on round stools or stood. We held rice bowls and scooped jiaozi into our mouths with our chopsticks. The fifteen of us nearly filled the small room.

I sat by one of Jason's cousins who was about ten years old. We made conversation of English nouns she was learning at school.

"Socks," she said, pointing to her feet.

I grabbed a lock of my hair. "Hair."

"Shirt."

"Eyes."

"Nose."

Riveting conversation it was not, but in my present surroundings I couldn't complain about anything that was this easy.

I drank my third glass of 7-Up. Jason's uncle filled my glass with something that smelled like beer. I nudged Jason. "Can you tell them I don't drink?"

Jason sighed. "I will try."

He spoke to the uncle in Chinese which merely made the uncle pour Jason a glass too.

"My uncle says you can try."

"I don't want to try it. I don't want to drink."

Jason nodded. "I know this, Daniel. This is very hard in China."

Jason spoke to his uncle some more in Chinese.

"Uncle wants to know why you do not drink."

"Well, you know, Jason. I'm a Christian, and I don't think drinking is a good way to honor God. But if your uncle doesn't know much about Christianity, that isn't really the place I want to begin to explain it."

"I know this. Always this uncle give me pressure to drink alcohol. He does not like to hear 'no.'"

I reached to pull a few squares off the roll of toilet paper on the table. These were napkins that never needed folding. I dabbed at my fingers, stalling for time. "Tell him I'm too young."

"He gives it to his son which is fourteen."

"Then tell him my parents won't let me. Will he listen to that?"

"I will try."

Jason explained some more. Some of the other uncles joined in the argument. Several minutes later Daniel's dad muttered some words, and they left us alone.

"I'm glad you are here," Jason whispered. "Because you are my friend, I think Uncle will not force me to drink."

The meal did finally end. Jason's dad turned the volume up on the TV. This special TV broadcast seemed to be China's way of seeing in the New Year. Acrobats performed stunts. Singers sang. Comedians gave long Chinese monologues. It was going to be a long night.

Once the broadcast started, firecrackers started in earnest. Cigarette smoke choked the air. The bottle of booze came around again and again. Men especially were pressured to drink more and more. I spent my evening pretending to watch TV.

At one point a commercial came on, and Jason's slightly tipsy policeman uncle singled me out. "Wu Dan," he said, but I couldn't follow any of the Chinese after my name.

Jason's dad eyed me. "He say you American, you Christian. Yes?"

I nodded.

"He say you teach Li Jing religion. Yes?"

I nodded.

"He say you teach us religion."

I looked at Jason. His eyes lit up. "Yes, Daniel. You must tell my family about the Bible. You can use Chinese or you can use English and I will translate."

I had hoped, during my time here, to find a good opportunity to witness to Jason's family. But somehow I never pictured this. I had thought maybe I could witness quietly to his parents someday if they seemed ready to listen. Speaking to the extended family who had shown no interest in the Gospel hadn't entered my mind. And I had asked God to give me some sort of sign that it was an appropriate time and place—something more than the drunken request of their policeman uncle.

TWELVE

I had looked forward to preaching my first sermon, but I never expected it to be like this.

Jason's family displayed various stages of drunkenness. The only thing louder than the TV was the deafening explosion of firecrackers.

Chuck's three questions sprinted through my mind. Did I know these people? Jason, yes, but none of his family. Genuine spiritual interest? Not much of that. Appropriate time and place? I didn't know much about Jason's family, but his uncle was a policeman.

Every eye turned to me. Jason gazed at me like I was Gabriel himself.

Well, Lord, I prayed. *I can't even see my comfort zone from here. I don't know where to begin. But Jason brought me here to witness to his family and I just can't say nothing. Fill my mouth with the right words.*

I started in Chinese, though I knew it wouldn't last long. "To Chinese people, New Year's is the most important holiday. To Americans, Christmas is the most important holiday."

Jason's dad asked in English, "Christmas is Western New Year. Is it true?"

"No. January first is the American New Year's. Christmas is Jesus Christ's birthday." My Chinese ran out, and Jason had to translate. I'd tell them the same stuff I told William. "*Yesu Jidu*, Jesus Christ, is God's Son. Jesus was born to a poor family. He died thirty-three years later. Christians believe Jesus became alive again. We believe He now lives with His Father in heaven."

Jason's father frowned. He held up two fingers. "Father, Son. How many gods Americans worship?"

"We worship one God Who created the world. He sent His Son Jesus to the earth to make peace between God and men—kind of like a matchmaker or go-between."

Jason translated and added a few words of his own about Chinese go-betweens.

Chinese acrobats jumped across the TV screen catching the attention of several family members.

Jason's father worked at forming his thoughts in English. "Go-between take care of problem. What problem God have?"

He asked in English. I had to try to explain it in English. "God is holy. That means He never does bad things. He only does good things. God hates bad things. Bad things are sin. God cannot love sin or people with sin. God made the father and mother of all people. He made us. God loves people and wants to be their friend, but their sin, the bad things they do, makes this impossible."

"Impossible." Mr. Li considered the word. "No person can do impossible. How Jesus do?"

"Jesus is good. I am bad. God says bad people must die. Jesus did not need to die. Jesus died so people do not need to die."

Mr. Li switched back into Chinese. He had never heard of a person who didn't die. Could Jesus really do something to us so we wouldn't die? Thankfully Jason explained to him the difference between physical death and spiritual death. By now the rest of the family was watching TV again.

Mr. Li shook his head. "In China, go-between want much money. How much money Jesus want?"

"Jesus didn't want any money. He loves all people. He wants them to be friends with God."

"Jesus want no money? Jesus die, make peace with God and man. Is it true?"

"Yes, Mr. Li. Jesus died in our place, instead of us, so we could be God's friends."

"Die for people very hard, very big thing. Jesus think peace with God very important?"

"Yes. Jesus died . . . a very painful death. It was not easy. But Jesus loved people very much."

"Li Jing is Christian. Before I not understand this. Now maybe I understand why Li Jing love Jesus."

Yet another string of firecrackers exploded outside. It was close to the house, louder than the others. The sound nearly jolted me from my chair, but no one else seemed to notice. I glanced back at Mr. Li, but he seemed to be following the TV comedian.

I couldn't help but wonder what it would be like to know absolutely nothing about God. Then you find out that God is powerful enough to create the world and the people in it, yet He wants to be your friend. It seems like an impossible friendship until you find out His Son can make it work. The Son thought this friendship was so important that He died to make it happen. He doesn't charge for the effort. He offers free salvation.

How many thousands of times had I heard that truth presented? Now in my stumbling Chinese and my first-grade English vocabulary I had explained this truth to Jason's family for the very first time. Wow.

Hour after hour I stared at the TV screen, pretending interest in the never-ending New Year's special. I fought to keep my eyes open, but I could not regret coming. I would never forget Mr. Li's words: "I think maybe I understand why Li Jing love Jesus."

Sometime after midnight Jason's aunt and uncles went home. By then Jason's grandmother had claimed her bed. Eventually Jason's parents took the other bed. Jason and I rolled a thin, narrow mat onto the floor and tried to sleep. Waves of firecrackers exploded in a ceaseless lullaby.

I woke a few hours later to the sound of Mrs. Li rattling around in the kitchen. It didn't matter that I was nowhere near ready to get up. I was sleeping in the family room and my room was needed. For the good of the family I got up.

I slipped into the bathroom, undressed, and hung my clothes and towel on the one hook in the room. Showering demanded full concentration as I had to avoid spraying my clothes or stepping into the Chinese toilet. Too hot water alternated with too cold as it trickled out of the ancient plumbing.

What would we do today? It was a Chinese holiday, so this first day I would have to step back and let the family observe their various customs. Then the rest of the week maybe Jason and I could choose to do things we enjoyed more.

Or so I thought. I had lived in China for five months, but I soon learned that I had only skimmed the surface of Chinese culture. My first clue came at breakfast.

Jason's grandmother ladled some *tangyuan* balls into my bowl. I pinched one with my chopsticks and stuck it in my mouth, biting through the chewy exterior to the brown sugar inside. "So, Jason, what are the plans for today?"

Jason poured me some tea. "I will take care of you Daniel. You don't have to worry."

I wasn't worried. I just wanted to psych myself up to fit into a very different world than normal. "I know that. I just thought . . . well, it might be nice to know what we are going to do."

"We will do many interesting things. You will see the real China during Chinese New Year's. I am so excited my family can meet you."

Was it an insult to wonder what you were going to do that day? It wouldn't be to an American, but I was a long way from America.

Jason and I joined the rest of the Li family as they roamed the village in their new outfits, greeting friends and relatives. I was possibly the only foreigner in the whole village, which made me an interesting conversation piece, but an unimportant rung on the village ladder.

Everywhere we walked I nodded to strangers and gave the traditional New Year's greeting, "*Gong xi fa cai.*"

The first red envelope startled me. Jason's second uncle presented it to me. I knew enough to accept it with both hands, a nod, and a thank you. Jason stuck his in his pocket, so I did the same. Red envelopes meant money. Why would Jason's relatives give me money?

In time we edged out of the conversation. Jason led me behind a crumbling concrete wall. "You must not look in envelope when person give to you. That is not polite. You must wait until they are not looking."

Jason peeked in his envelope, so I peeked in mine. Fifty yuan! It was worth over six US dollars. In this village it was a lot of money. I was still struggling with the poverty of this village. The last thing I wanted was money from these people.

"Jason, I don't expect your family to give me red envelopes. It's really nice of them to allow me to share the holiday with you, but I'm just here to watch. I mean, you're one of their family, so if that's what they do at New Year's, that's fine. But I don't want them to give anything to me."

Jason smiled. It was the way he smiled when he was embarrassed that I had said too much about something. "You are our guest, Daniel. Of course they will give you red envelopes."

"You think others will give me red envelopes too?"

"Do not worry, Daniel. You are in China now. We Chinese say, 'When you go to a foreign place, you must follow local custom.'"

Right. The Chinese when-in-Rome saying.

By the end of the day I had collected fifteen red envelopes with a total of three hundred fifty yuan. Each time another Chinese adult pulled another red envelope out of his pocket, I prayed, *Please, Lord, help me accept this gift graciously although I am wealthy by their standards.*

We spent the day listening to Chinese conversations which I barely understood. It made an interesting study in Chinese New Year's customs, but the day passed slowly.

Tuesday morning I was definitely ready to go out and do something. Jason dished me up some watery rice for breakfast and added some green vegetables.

I tried not to ask, but the words jumped out of my mouth. "What do you think we will do today?"

"Do not worry, Daniel. I will take care of everything."

That again. If I couldn't choose what we did, it would be nice at least to know what we'd be doing. Maybe Jason was still working out plans.

Sometime after the dishes were washed, Jason informed me that his aunt and her son were taking us to a tea plantation. That sounded pretty good. The aunt showed up and we strolled toward town to catch a taxi. I would have been glad to ride a pedicab, but his aunt said that it was New Year's, and we must celebrate.

We waited on a dusty corner. Before an empty taxi could drive by, the aunt's friend joined us. Jason introduced me to Auntie Mei, who wasn't really related at all. The two women carried on a lively conversation while a taxi sped by. Their voices grew louder and louder until a pedicab pulled up. The five of us squeezed in.

"The pedicab is a good idea," I told Jason. The expense of the taxi embarrassed me. "I don't mind taking a pedicab to the tea plantation."

Jason flashed his embarrassed smile. "We're not going to the tea plantation now. Auntie Mei says we should go fishing. She says Americans like fishing."

This American wasn't crazy about fishing, but at least it would get us out in the country—or so I thought. We pulled up to a cement pond in a ring of rice paddies and tin buildings. The vendor handed us each bamboo poles with line and fish hooks at one end. He explained that we would pay for the fish we caught by weight. I prayed that if I caught a fish it would be a small one. Someone would have to pay for it, and I was absolutely sure it wouldn't be me.

And so it went every day. I never knew ahead of time what we were going to do. I began to realize Jason didn't either. Once we decided what to do, a relative or friend of a friend would come along, and we would end up doing what that person wanted us to do. Choosing anything would have been a luxury. Even knowing what we were going to do would have helped. My American brain worked on an inner clock and compass. Once I had a basic idea of what was going on, I could enjoy a certain amount of adventure. But this constant uncertainty about what we would do next left me feeling disoriented, unprepared, out of control.

Wednesday it was Jason's uncle's turn to treat. We stuffed the uncle's family, Jason's family, and several neighbors into two taxis and rode to a lookout point on the mountain. A yak dressed in pink ornaments seemed to be the main attraction. Jason's uncle paid to have our picture taken with the yak. On the mountain we met a friend of the family who took us to her brother's jade factory. I felt compelled to buy a few souvenirs which Jason insisted on paying for.

Thursday Jason's neighbor took us to a tea plantation where we met the neighbor's former classmate. She insisted we see an ancient temple nearby which took us in another direction.

Friday Jason and I had started playing basketball at the village basketball hoop when we met a former classmate of Jason's. He was the mayor's son. I'm not sure how it happened, but we ended the day sitting on a rented boat in a lake eating melon seeds with the mayor.

By Saturday morning I was more than ready to go home to Huajiang. Soft green mountains lined with rice patties and tea plantations formed a beautiful backdrop to this village—if you could just block out the shabby buildings in the foreground. But after five days I couldn't block out the negative things any longer. I tried to not to stare, but I was sure we had passed several houses made of mud bricks with tin roofs.

My internal clock and compass were also flashing their warning lights. I had never thought of myself as a control freak, but right now I desperately wanted to go home and make my own decisions. I would choose predictable oatmeal over adventure every time. Could I stand twenty-four hours more of being pushed from place to place by generous strangers?

I grabbed my clothes and headed for the tiny bathroom. After five days I had mastered the art of hanging all my clothes on the one hook. I missed my Western toilet and our shower with a tub and a shower curtain to contain the water. I turned on the water and prayed. "One more day, Lord. Just give me grace for one more day."

At breakfast we ate watery rice. I told Jason I was getting pretty tired. "Maybe we should stay around your home today."

Jason smiled in embarrassment. "I am sorry to make you tired Daniel. Living in such poor conditions is hard for you."

"It's just that, well, usually I get more sleep than I have this week."

"I am sorry. My home is not comfortable. But my father's friend promise he will take us to restaurant tonight. He hire my father teach extra classes at his school. I think we must go with him tonight. If we do not go, my father will lose face."

Once more the choice had been made, and I must flex or offend. But the day was not a total loss. That noon I finally ate lunch with just Jason, his parents, and his grandmother. Jason's mom fixed simple vegetables on rice. In China, simple was good. It was the delicacies which were hard to stomach.

I knew I would never find a better time to thank Jason's parents for inviting me. It had been a wearing week, one I would not want to repeat soon. But this country family had been very generous to me on an extremely limited budget.

I ate quietly, working out the Chinese words in my head. "Thank you for inviting me to come to your house to celebrate Chinese New Year's. Your son is a very good friend to me."

Jason's family waved my comments away as if they had done nothing. Typical Chinese reaction.

I could tell Mr. Li was working out English in his head the same way I had done with my Chinese. "We very happy you Li Jing's friend. Li Jing very lucky have American teacher be friend."

I stuck with English. "Li Jing has taught me many things about China and Chinese culture. I can learn to speak Chinese at school, but Li Jing has taught me things I could never learn at school."

Jason didn't even look up. "It is nothing, Daniel."

"It is important to me. Please translate for me and tell your family."

Jason mumbled some quick Chinese.

Mr. Li shook his head. "Li Jing is only son. Her . . . his English very poor. You help him."

"I think Li Jing has very good English. His English is much better than my Chinese."

"No. Very poor. I think Li Jing must learn good English. No good English, no success. Family always poor."

"I'm glad to help him. We are friends. We can help each other."

"Jason very lucky have foreigner friend. Before . . ." Mr. Li frowned and left his English behind leaving Jason to translate.

"During Cultural Revolution foreigners very few. Government say Chinese cannot speak to foreigners. My father say every person have little freedom. Now it is much better. Before Cultural Revolution my family had more money. Then nothing. Very poor. Just watery rice every day. No meat. Now better. My father says I am only hope in future for them. Maybe you see why they think it is important you be my friend."

Grandmother Li burst into the conversation with a staccato voice and wide gestures.

Jason translated. "Grandmother say when she was small girl, Americans live in her village. They were missionaries. Sunday they teach class for children. Every Sunday she go to class. Missionary woman put special pictures on board and tell stories. Missionary woman was very kind. Her Chinese was strange, but she give candy to children and speak kind words to them."

Grandmother Li continued chattering, waving her arms and shaking her head.

"When Grandmother was teenager government tell them, 'Hate America, love China.' Government say must not trust foreigners. Grandmother cannot talk to missionaries. Some people very bad to missionaries. But Grandmother remember missionary woman was very kind, though her Chinese was poor."

Jason listened some more.

"Grandmother say her friend's daughter is Li Huo. Remember, I told you about her? She is Christian. She lives in Beijing now. Li Huo say she hear in big city like Beijing today, there are some missionaries again—like before."

I coughed. "Really?"

"Grandmother say, do you know, is it true?"

Had Jason never guessed that *I* was a missionary? Chuck said that he never told our Chinese friends that he was a missionary. It was better to let them have their guesses than to remove all doubt.

I cleared my throat. "Well, I know that there used to be many missionaries in China. I've read books about them. But now the government doesn't want missionaries to come to China. The government would rather have teachers and lawyers and engineers and stuff like that."

Jason translated.

Chopsticks clicked loudly in the sudden silence. Jason's grandmother leaned close to him and whispered.

Jason leaned close to me. "Grandmother say when she was teenager her best friend become Christian. That time Grandmother want to become Christian too, but if she talk to foreigners, bring

126

danger. Grandmother know missionaries' talk about God is true, but Grandmother is afraid if she become Christian must face big trouble. Grandmother always want to believe, always afraid. She never talk about this to anyone."

I felt honored to be in on this new revelation.

Jason continued. "When I ask parents if I may get baptized, they think it is not good. They say Christian succeed is hard. But Grandmother tell them, 'If Jason want to be Christian, do not stop him. Success can be good or can be bad. Believe as person wants is very good. Today in China be Christian is sometimes hard, but much easy than before.'"

"Tell your grandmother that it is not too late for her. She can become a Christian now."

Jason whispered to his grandmother.

"Grandmother say she already choose road, cannot change now."

I wanted to say, "You can too change! All of you can become Christians. I can tell you how. You can pray the sinner's prayer, and I can lead my first person—my first people—to Christ. Then this whole uncomfortable week, even my whole time in China, will be worth it all. Then I will know that God can use me as a missionary."

But that would be too much, too soon. Jason and I had witnessed to his family. His grandmother had heard some of this years ago. For everyone else it was the first time they had heard that the God Who created the world had sent His Son to die for us. They needed to learn more before they would be ready to believe. I hadn't said much, but it was a beginning. For now, it was enough.

THIRTEEN

In a way I was the guest of honor at dinner that night. At least Mr. Li's friend used me as an excuse to invite Jason's family. He wanted to show the foreigner the best restaurant in Zhushan. Or perhaps he wanted to show Zhushan that he had a connection to the foreigner. But I didn't know half of the people at the table, and most of them didn't know English. I got too much attention one minute and was totally forgotten the next. I preferred the latter.

Tinsel ornaments and suggestive pictures of American movie stars hung on the walls. The waitress seated us at a round table on stacking stools. Our host, Mr. Wei, carried on a loud conversation with Mr. Li. The waitress poured beer into all the glasses. Mr. Wei turned to me and raised his glass. "To our American friend."

"Help me, Jason," I whispered. "I can't drink that."

Jason apologized profusely for me in Chinese and asked if we could have some tea.

Mr. Wei found this hilarious. He laughed loudly exposing a mouth full of stained teeth. He glanced knowingly around the table, making comments about the naïve foreigner who couldn't drink beer. He directed another comment to Jason.

Jason leaned over to me. "He says you can try it and see if you like it. He says we won't tell your parents."

"Look, Jason, you know I don't want to be rude, but I'm not going to drink that. Can't you just tell him that, I don't know, that I've visited the tea plantation and want to remember drinking tea with you or something?"

Jason grinned with embarrassment and offered some sort of explanation. Jason's grandmother rarely said much, but she chose this moment, bless her, to speak up. It was something about the foreigner honoring them by preferring the local tea to beer. I could have kissed her toothless, old mouth—well, almost.

The waitress poured tea for Jason and me and his grandmother. A few others asked for it too. I didn't know if they were trying to make me feel comfortable, or if my brazen refusal to drink had simply helped them to decline.

Glasses of beer and tea were raised again to "their American friend." Having toasted me I was largely forgotten for some time. The waitress brought melon seeds while Mr. Wei ordered the rest of the meal. I cracked the shells with my teeth and attempted to keep up a little conversation in my limited Chinese.

Several more groups crowded into the tiny restaurant until some groups shared tables with others.

Bowls of food started to arrive: egg drop soup, spicy vegetables, fried noodles, an eel dish. I hated to think what this meal was costing our host. I picked at this and that until the waitress presented us with a dish meant to impress the foreigner.

Our host grinned and rattled off fast Chinese for Jason to translate.

Jason leaned close. "Mr. Wei says this dish is, how do you say it? This dish is specialty of restaurant. It is rabbit head."

I gazed at the plate. Thankfully it was cooked well enough that the parts were not clearly distinguishable. I held my chopsticks over my plate. That part must be the rabbit's brain. Perhaps that other part was his cheek. Where did you begin with something like this?

Mr. Wei smiled, waiting for me to try some rabbit head. He spoke again.

Jason translated. "He say eat and enjoy."

Which did he want me to do—eat or enjoy? *Both* were impossible. The whole table watched as I chose a bit of meat which was most likely rabbit cheek and bit into it. It wasn't easy, but I smiled.

Mr. Wei reached across with his chopsticks and dragged some of the brain into my bowl.

I could understand his Chinese. "Try it."

Lord, help me, I prayed. I choked the brain meat down, but excused myself within a few minutes and hurried to the restroom to throw up. That made me feel better, but I knew I still had to go out and face Jason's friends and family.

The meal finally ended. Longing for home, even Jason's home, my heart sank when the host insisted we go to the karaoke place in town.

Smoke choked the air in the crowded KTV room. Mr. Wei handed me a microphone and asked me what song I wanted to sing.

I hollered to Jason over the noise. "Tell him I can't read Chinese. I will just watch."

Jason argued back and forth with Mr. Wei, then turned to me. "He say they have English songs. He want to hear our foreigner friend sing English song."

"I don't know many popular songs," I told him. "I do more with classical music."

In the end Jason picked out a song and the two of us sang, "Catch a falling star and put it in your pocket." After that Mr. Wei handed the microphone to someone else and forced him to sing. The smoke, crowd, and deafening noise made my head throb.

One of the strangers in our group brought over a Chinese girl to introduce to me. She seemed to be a cousin of his who happened to be at the KTV the same time we were. "Jasmine" wore a tight top, short skirt, and high heels.

As we were introduced, Jasmine struck a flirty pose. She seemed to be standing a little too close to me, but I was leaning against a wall and unable to move.

Jasmine rattled off something in her fractured country dialect.

Jason glanced at me apologetically. "Jasmine want me to ask you if you have girlfriend."

I frowned. "Tell her that I am not looking for a girlfriend right now, because I have more important things to do in China."

Jason translated to giggles all around.

"Jasmine say what thing is so important you cannot have girlfriend."

This was ridiculous. Something in me wanted to shout, "I'm here as a missionary, if it's any of your business!" What could I say instead? "Tell her that my father teaches English, and I want to use my last year at home to learn about China and spend time with my family."

I waited for a response. "Jasmine say some foreigners refuse to marry Chinese girl. Do you think same way?"

I massaged my throbbing temples. How could anyone think over this noise? "Tell her I don't want to marry anyone for a long time."

In Huajiang I knew what to do in a case like this. In Huajiang, rude or not, I would excuse myself, call a taxi, and go home. But I wasn't in Huajiang.

Jason looked annoyed himself. "Jasmine say people say Americans marry for love. She want to know if you think marry for love is important, or if marry for money is OK too."

"Listen Jason," I said. "I'm really not feeling well. Is there any way we could go home soon?"

Jason's embarrassed smile was back. "I am sorry, Daniel. I know this is not good place. I want to go home, but this year Mr. Wei did big favor for my father. I think leave so soon is rude."

FOURTEEN

Sunday morning was never my first choice for travel time, but it was the only time Jason could get me a train ticket home.

On the train I bought a bowl of noodles from a lady with a loud, grating voice. A week ago I would have said her outfit didn't match, but after a week in Zhushan it didn't look so bad. I drank the broth from the bowl, then slurped the noodles into my mouth straight from the bowl. I didn't have a napkin or even the little pack of toilet paper I usually carried, so I wiped my mouth on my sleeve.

I wasn't exactly missing church. Jason didn't know of any churches in his village. If Zhushan had a church of any kind, it was very well hidden.

I thought about that as I held onto the baggage rack of the moving train. Jason got saved in our little house church in Huajiang. When he went home, he not only didn't have a church to attend, he didn't even know one Christian in Zhushan. If someone in his family did get saved, they would be on their own with no Christian support.

Compared to Jason, I was rich, and I wasn't just thinking about money. Yet Jason was the most thankful person I knew.

Since I was returning to Huajiang on my own, I kept my mouth shut on the train. The trip would be much easier if no one knew I spoke any Chinese. Usually I appreciated opportunities to use my Chinese, but this week I had used every bit of energy I possessed. Now I just wanted to get home.

What a week! Zhushan was a giant step down from Huajiang. And Huajiang was a big step down from Seattle. It reminded me of Jesus' step down from heaven to a carpenter's home. OK. Compared to Jesus I hadn't stepped down very far, but it was a big step down for me.

The train lurched to a stop. I slammed into the lady standing next to me. She didn't even look up.

How could I feel so drained after a week of doing almost nothing? Everyone had been kind to me, more than generous. The food was different from my usual, but most of it was pretty good. Yet somehow I had lost my identity. In a crowd I was the stupid one who couldn't speak much Chinese. No one needed my ideas in Jason's village. No one consulted me when they were making plans. No one allowed me to pay for anything. I had spent my whole week following people around, trying not to offend anyone. I had no control over anything.

Control. I wanted to choose. I wanted other people to do what I suggested for a change. I wanted to share my American ideas and show all the Chinese how superior those ideas were.

I liked American ways. In America, when guests came to our house, we told them to make themselves at home, and to ask if they needed anything. When we went on outings, we let the guests choose where they wanted to go. If they wanted to pay their own way, we rarely stopped them. It was our way of making them feel comfortable, of giving choices and respecting individual differences.

Individuality—that's what they needed in China.

I scrunched up my paper noodle bowl, stuck it in a plastic bag and tied it shut. I pushed the whole thing into my backpack. I wasn't going to litter like some of the Chinese I had seen. Americans would know better than to throw all this trash around.

An elderly Chinese lady tapped me on the back. She held out her own personal trash bag and pointed to my backpack. I could add my trash to hers.

"Xie xie." I pulled my trash back out and added it to hers. *And thank you, Lord for the reminder to listen to myself,* I prayed. Who was this control freak who had to have his way? Who was this judgmental person who just knew American ways were better than Chinese?

Chuck had said something once about the way Americans and Chinese think. Americans stress the importance of being an individual while Chinese think more of the needs of the group. Before this week I had only guessed at what that meant. Maybe I was beginning to understand. Generosity was important. Choice was not.

Jason constantly gave up his wishes for the good of the group. But I knew better. With my supposedly superior American thinking and eleven years of being a Christian, I knew just enough to want my own way. I prayed, "Lord, help me to learn from the new believers around me."

I kept thinking about this culture stuff the whole week after I got home. Before New Year's I wanted to learn more about Chinese culture so I could understand my Chinese friends better. I guess I was really wanting to know a *little* more about Chinese culture so that I could understand them a *little* better. During my five months in China I had gotten to know Chinese people in very controlled settings at our Bible studies or in our home. I had spent time with Jason and William, but mainly one on one, with them trying to please me. Actually living in a Chinese family in a Chinese village was so much more than that. I had had enough of Chinese culture to last me a while. I didn't want to go anywhere.

I ate oatmeal everyday. Mom cooked the most American food she could find in Huajiang. It took a whole week of predictability to make me interested in adventure again.

Then William invited me to a Chinese concert. Colorful lanterns bordered the walkway to the concert hall. Tiger lanterns were most popular since we were beginning the year of the tiger. After dark the lanterns would be lit for the lantern festival.

William found us seats not far from the orchestra. He pointed out the various Chinese instruments as they began to warm up. I spotted the pipa with its fat round body and slender neck. The *ruan* looked a lot like a banjo. Some of the Chinese instruments were similar to the violins, flutes, oboes and trumpets we had in our orchestra in Seattle.

About two o'clock William had just started explaining facts about Chinese music when a friend of his named Brandon found us. Brandon was in the same class as William and Jason, but clearly outclassed William with his knowledge of music. He told me the Chinese and English name of every instrument. He had played the *xun*, a round clay sort of flute, in an orchestra once. He pointed out the *morin khur*, a two stringed violin of which the neck, for some strange reason, stretched into a carved horse head.

Brandon explained some of the differences between Western music and Chinese music. I'm sure he could have talked for hours if the music hadn't started.

I enjoyed the unusual music—for the first hour. Then the discordant sounds, and noisy gongs and drums began to get on my nerves. When the concert finished at 3:45, I was more than ready to leave.

Brandon asked me if I had ever eaten tangyuan. I told him I had eaten the sweet, chewy rice balls at Jason's house. That didn't satisfy Brandon. He knew where they made the best tangyuan in Huajiang. He said we must try them. William put on his most humble expression. "I am very sorry, Brandon. You are very good friend to invite us, but we cannot go. My mother say we must come home very quick. She prepare early meal for us because we go to lantern festival tonight. If we be late, mother is angry."

I gave my apologies, and William and I started for the bus stop.

I frowned. "I thought the two of us were going to a noodle shop for supper."

"Yes, Daniel we will go."

"But you told Brandon . . ."

William waved away my concern. "Brandon sometimes is very boring. I do not want to force you to listen to him talk for long time on music. You are polite, but Brandon never stop."

Was it my imagination or was William jealous of Brandon's knowledge of music? "So what you told Brandon . . . that is not true?"

"To be true, I do not like Brandon very much, but I must be polite. Brandon's mother work for visa department. Someday I need her help."

I suppose I should have been glad that we didn't have another stranger planning our evening. Jason would let anyone change our plans. But after spending a week with Jason I had come to expect more. More of William. Maybe more of myself too.

When we got to William's house, his mom was still at work. It was too early to eat. Mr. Wang was dressed for some social engagement. He grabbed his car keys as we walked in the door. He asked about the concert. When William told him about meeting Brandon, Mr. Wang's eyes glowed with approval.

"Daniel, you are a good friend to help William with his English."

"I don't mind. That's what friends are for. William helps me too. He takes me lots of places and helps me know my way around Huajiang."

"It is nothing. William is so lucky to have a native English speaker to teach him English. He must improve his English so he can pass the TOEFL test. Brandon's mother can help William get a student visa for America, but William must pass the TOEFL test first."

"William has very good English for a Chinese person his age. He should do all right."

Mr. Wang shook his head. "William is very lazy. Two times already he has taken the TOEFL test. Last time his score was 452. He must get 525 to pass."

"I'm sure the test isn't easy. He almost passed the test. I wouldn't begin to pass that kind of test if they had one in Chinese."

Mr. Wang clutched his car keys in a tight fist. "*Almost* passing the TOEFL test doesn't help him at all! All his life I sent William to English classes. I paid big money. Still he does not succeed. I am the head of the English department at Huajiang Normal University. What will people think if my lazy son cannot pass TOEFL?"

I studied the rug, avoiding Mr. Wang's glaring eyes. "William doesn't really seem lazy to me. I think he tries very hard. Learning another language isn't easy."

"If William wanted to pass the TOEFL, he could. I have paid for many tutors. He must study abroad so he can be a successful businessman. His mother and I didn't have the advantages William has. We had to work very hard to achieve our positions. William must work hard, or what will happen to our family? We only have one son. If he fails we have no hope."

William hung his head in humiliation. I wasn't going to win this argument, so I dropped it. Chinese were naturally modest. They rarely accepted compliments. But Mr. Wang's criticism was more than just modesty.

Suddenly the fire in Mr. Wang's eyes died and a polite smile flickered across his face. He told us goodbye and left.

William pulled a Go game out of the cabinet and set the board on the glass coffee table. Tears quivered in his eyes threatening to spill onto his face, but he turned away to search for M&M's and rubbed his eyes on his sleeve.

"Look William, I like your dad and everything, but I think he's wrong about you. English is not easy for a Chinese person. I don't think you're lazy. I think you just have to keep working."

"My father think he must shame me become better student. I must try harder."

"How many hours do you study every day?"

William pulled two bags of M&M's from the cupboard. "Every week I go to class thirty hours. In evening I study, but only study until midnight. Sunday my tutor help me. Saturday I study only part of day. Sometime go with you, do fun thing, forget about study. It is not enough! I must work harder! I must success!"

"Succeed." The word was out before I could stop it.

"What do you say?"

"Succeed is the verb. You must succeed. You must be a success."

"I know this. I try but it is never good enough."

"I'm sorry, William. My parents just tell me to do my best. As long as I do that, it is good enough. But I don't think your father agrees."

"Your parents do not pressure you?"

"Not really."

"That is American thinking."

"Yes, I suppose it is an American thing."

William moved the Go markers and adjusted the game board. "Is that a Christian thing too?"

I sighed. William needed to know this. How could I not tell him? "Yes, William, it is a Christian thing. We don't have to work to win God's favor."

"I do not understand."

"OK. God has a very high standard. We can never be good enough for Him—at least not by ourselves. But His Son Jesus was good enough, even perfect. Jesus was . . . good in our place. With Jesus as our friend God will accept us."

I hadn't even mentioned sin, but how could I bring sin up when his dad had already humiliated him?

The clock ticked loudly for several minutes. Finally William broke the silence. "I would like to believe in God like that, but I must work to success, to succeed, for my family."

"You can work to succeed and believe in God too."

"For you this is easy. For me, no. My father say I should join Communist Party. Communism and Christian do not mix together. If Communist, I must follow Communism thinking. I must stand by flag, promise to serve Communism."

"Did your dad say you must join the Party? Is it that important to him?"

"He say if I join Party, I get good job. Join Party help me in very many ways. I am not good student. I am only average. How can I succeed if I do not join Party?"

What could I say? Even though he was eighteen, I wanted to encourage William to obey his father. But Max was a Party member, and now that he was saved one thing seemed clear. If there was a reasonable way to get out of the Party, he would do it. William's comment, "Communism and Christian do not mix together," was an understatement.

William handed me the white markers for the Go game. "I'm sorry Daniel. Be Christian is good thing for you, but I think for me, be Christian is too hard."

FIFTEEN

A white board eraser sailed across the Chinese classroom and hit me on the ear. I usually like holidays, but I was glad the New Year's holiday was over. March had come and with it my normal Chinese class with the same few guys who liked to toss stuff around the room.

I picked up the eraser. I could hurl it back at the European student and join the game, but I had never seen erasers defy gravity in regular Chinese classrooms.

Liu Laoshi watched anxiously from the other side of the room. Last year I had openly declared, "I am a Christian." Since then I tried to be pretty careful about what I did in this class. Now I was trying to be more sensitive to cultural issues. This was one party I could do without.

I crossed the room and handed the eraser to Liu Laoshi. I nodded, gave my normal greeting. "Laoshi, *ni hao*."

She nodded back, returned my greeting, accepted the eraser with thankful eyes. Maybe it was unnecessary, personally greeting my teacher before every day of classes, but Brittany always did it. She also thanked Liu Laoshi for teaching us each day before she left. Since Brittany thought that was important, I had decided it couldn't hurt.

After a few minutes class settled down. We finished one lesson, then repeated vocabulary words from the next after Liu Laoshi. Then came whole sentences in Chinese.

> My favorite subject is math.
> My favorite subject is English.
> My favorite subject is geography.
> My favorite subject is history.
> My favorite subject is science.

Adam scribbled on the side of his book. "Boring."

> I like to read stories. I also like to write stories.
> I like to study about other countries. We can learn from history.
> I like to study about animals. Science teaches us how the world began. Long ago people evolved from monkeys.

Adam's book slid to the floor. He shook himself awake and retrieved it. He must have had another late night last night.

We practiced repeating the phrases after Liu Laoshi. She called on several people to tell about their favorite subjects. I buried my head in my book.

The bell rang. Most of the students ambled out into the hallway for the morning break. I hung behind. Liu Laoshi usually helped students who stayed behind practice their Chinese.

She closed her book and slipped over to my desk.

"Wu Dan, do you like to study at home?" she asked in Chinese.

"Yes. Because I study at home, I have more time than ordinary students. I can see many things in Huajiang."

"What is your favorite subject?"

"My favorite subject is science."

"Do you like to study about how the world began?"

I cleared my throat. "Yes."

Liu Laoshi glanced around the room. The closest person sat on the far side. She slipped into English. "I have heard that Christians do not believe people evolved from monkeys. Is this true?"

I nodded. "Yes. That's true."

"Long ago I told you I read Genesis in the Bible. It says God made the earth in six days. Every person comes from the first man and woman. Do you believe that?"

"Yes."

"Scientists say that the earth is billions of years in age. You don't believe that, do you?"

"No."

"How can you disagree with science?" She studied my face with curiosity, not anger.

"Not all scientists believe that the world is billions of years old. Many believe that the world could not have evolved from nothing. Even scientists don't agree on these things. When I look at all the animals and people, I see that they are, well, complicated. You know. Like when you study the human body and how it works together and how people can think and invent incredible things. It just seems like, well, it's pretty hard to believe that all of that just happened by chance."

"I see. We Chinese believe in evolution. Our schools tell us this is true." She slipped back into Chinese. "But I am only a Chinese teacher. I do not know about science."

She nodded and backed away.

OK, Lord, I prayed. *She started that conversation, so I have to believe You gave me that opportunity. I'm still a long way from sharing the Gospel, but I've only got three months before I leave China. Help me find a way to tell her more.*

Later I thought about Liu Laoshi's questions as I walked home. She was interested in creation science. We had some great books at home which gave good scientific reasons for believing the Bible's account of the world's origins. They explained why many scientists questioned the evidence for evolution. Liu Laoshi spoke good English, but she probably didn't know much scientific vocabulary. If only I could get a good book in Chinese that explained these things.

Wait. I remembered Chuck talking about some Christian books that questioned the credibility of evolution. They had been translated into Chinese. The books were part of a group of Christian books that were printed legally in China and on sale at certain bookstores. I would get a copy of one and bring it to Liu Laoshi.

The next day I located a bookstore and looked at what books were available. I was surprised at how many books they had. The titles and authors' names were in English as well as Chinese. I was sure I wouldn't agree with the doctrine in some of them, but others looked helpful. I chose one about Darwin, paid for it and left.

On the way home the bus wasn't as packed as usual. I sat in an actual seat and thanked God that China was now allowing some Christian books to be printed in Chinese and sold legally. I prayed that they would allow much more of this in the future.

On Wednesday I waited at the front of the classroom until Liu Laoshi walked into the room. Checking to see that no one was nearby I handed her the book in a brown paper bag. "I enjoyed talking to you the other day," I said. "I thought you might like to read this book."

Liu Laoshi nodded as she received the book with both hands. She slipped the package into her bag so smoothly I began to wonder if I had imagined giving it to her. "Xie xie, Wu Dan," she said and immediately began talking about the weather. She understood.

If I couldn't lead William to the Lord, maybe Liu Laoshi would become a Christian.

The time had gone so fast. I had learned so much about China, but what had I actually accomplished? Anything? Chuck must have sensed that I was anxious to do more. The next week he asked me to speak at the men's Bible study on Thursday evening.

It was my first sermon—not counting the one I preached to Jason's half-drunk relatives during the TV show. I was excited to lead a group Bible study on my own. But I wasn't going to impress anyone with my vast Bible knowledge. I didn't even want to. These guys were my friends.

Max had a great job, but he faced pressure at work to bribe officials and get around the law. He wanted to marry a Christian, but none of the Christian girls he knew were wealthy enough to please his parents.

Kenneth was married to an unbeliever who lived in Beijing. He was having health problems. Doctors had prescribed medicine but it wasn't helping.

Peter had come to our men's Bible study for several months. We weren't sure if he was a Christian or not. At twenty-three he still lived at home, but he didn't tell his parents he came to Bible studies because it would make them angry.

Cloudy had just started coming. His English wasn't very good. Like William he was studying long hours to pass the TOEFL test, but he wasn't doing very well.

Jason rarely mentioned his problems, but his life was far from easy.

What did I know about problems like this? I wouldn't even turn eighteen until next month. What could I say to make a difference?

Monday morning as I brushed my teeth I glared at the guy in the mirror. "Daniel, Daniel, Daniel," the foamy-mouthed reflection said. "Whatever will you speak about?" I rinsed my mouth with bottled water and spat into the sink. How could I help my friends live in an environment that hated God?

The answer fell like a golden rock from heaven's streets. I thanked the Lord and asked Him to help me say something worth listening to.

Thursday night our friends started appearing at our door. Our family was hosting the Bible study this week. Since the scare with Brittany's group, we had started moving our meetings around a bit. Unfortunately, our apartment building had tightened security and all our visitors had to sign in with the gate guard before they could come up. We were praying that this new measure wouldn't scare people away from meeting for Bible studies at our house.

Chuck, Richard, and Cloudy arrived early. Max's cell phone rang as soon as he sat down. Jason and Peter came about fifteen minutes late. Mom brought us all tea and disappeared into the bedroom. Kenneth had planned on coming, but we finally started without him. I played the guitar while we sang a couple of simple songs. Then Chuck said a few words and turned it over to me.

"I've lived in China more than seven months," I started. "I've learned a lot. I hope I've changed too and grown up a little. You guys really challenge me. Some of you are the only Christians in your whole families, and yet you work hard to live for God. You get so excited about the things you learn from the Bible. I want to be like that.

"In America we can go to . . ." I cleared my throat. Saying the C-word out loud in China seemed so wrong. "We can go to church any time we want. I have lots of Christian friends in America. I get used to that, and I don't appreciate it like I should. But God sees you here in China trying to please Him even when it's not easy.

"The Bible tells us about a guy named Daniel. When he was about my age, soldiers took him away from his home country. The new government didn't try to make him an atheist, you know, like in China when the schools want you to believe that there isn't any god. The government tried to make him worship false gods. I guess he's my favorite Bible character, partly because I'm named after him. Daniel had lots of pressure from the government not to worship God. He didn't fight the government, but he worked hard to find ways to please God and obey the government at the same time. Even though almost everyone around him worshiped false gods, Daniel stayed true to God.

"It wasn't easy for Daniel to live for God in the new country, but he decided he was going to obey God no matter how hard it was. He helped his friends to live for God too."

The doorbell buzzed. It was probably Kenneth. He often came late to men's Bible study. I asked the group to turn to the book of Daniel.

Dad opened the door. Were those green police uniforms? I shut my Bible and slid it under my chair. Dad shifted to one side, blocking the view from the doorway.

The extremely polite voice filtered across the room. "Excuse me, please. I am looking for Mr. Brett Wheeler, teacher at Huajiang Normal University."

"I'm Brett Wheeler."

They asked him to show his passport and he pulled it from his back pocket.

"Please, you must come with us to the office of the Public Security Bureau."

It was a chilly night, but Dad stepped out without his jacket and closed the door behind him. I wondered if the policemen had seen our quiet group of men with open Bibles on their laps.

SIXTEEN

I tiptoed to the bedroom door and opened it noiselessly. "Mom!" I whispered. "Some policemen just came to the door. They've taken Dad to the PSB for questioning!"

She whispered back, "Are they still here?"

"No, they're gone."

Mom rose from the bed where she had been reading and slipped into the living room. The circle of men watched us in silence, gauging our reaction. I could feel their thoughts. *These foreigners tell us to trust God. How do they react when trouble knocks on their door?*

Mom turned to Chuck. "Why do you think they took him? You weren't doing anything that would raise concerns, were you?"

Chuck shook his head. "Nothing unusual. We didn't even sing very loud. I have no idea why they would take Brett for questioning. We're more careful now than we have ever been."

"Did they say when he would get back? Did they give any clues about what they wanted?"

"Nothing. I guess we'll just have to wait and see what happens."

A neighbor's loud TV droned in the background. Jason broke the silence. "Excuse me Chuck. It is good time to pray, yes?"

"Yes, Jason. It is a very good time to pray."

I closed my eyes, but not before I noticed Jason. He folded his hands so tightly the knuckles turned white. His head hung low and his eyes were screwed shut too. I had taught him to pray this way. If I thought it would make a difference, I would fold my hands really tight too.

"Heavenly Father," Chuck prayed, "We know You are in control. We don't know why they are questioning Brett, but we know You can bring good out of this. Give him wise answers to their questions. Help him not to say anything that would endanger himself or his family or our group of believers. Help us too as we wait to hear what has happened. Help us to trust you."

Chuck prayed a few minutes longer, but my mind stopped with the trust part. *Yes, Lord*, I prayed. *Help me to trust You. Help Mom too. And help us to show these new believers what trust is.*

Peter turned to me. "Excuse me. I not know Bible much. To me it is new. May I ask, what happen in story?"

"What do you mean?"

He patted the Bible that still lay open on his lap. "What happen to Daniel? People force him not worship God. Did God save Daniel's life?"

I smiled. Perfect timing. I got to tell the story of Daniel and the lion's den to some who had never heard the story. In a few minutes I took Daniel from praying toward Jerusalem to hearing King Darius yell down into the den to see if he was still alive.

When I finished, Chuck suggested that it might be a good idea if the men left quietly, a few at a time.

Jason remained after the others left. "I can stay with you, Daniel."

I told him he didn't need to. I could worry better without him.

Jason slid his Bible into a little cloth bag and wriggled it into a corner of his backpack. "Daniel, I must ask question. In Bible did God always save life?"

I pictured John the Baptist's bloody head on a silver platter. Then stones striking Stephen, the first Christian martyr. Martyr was another M-word I tried not to think about.

"No, Jason. Sometimes people risked their lives, put their lives in danger, to obey God and God used a miracle to save them. But not always. Sometimes people died for Christ. It was a way to show God how much they loved him.

"Are you afraid, Daniel?"

My shoulder muscles were tensed into tight knots. I could not lie to Jason, even if I wanted to.

"I guess I am a little afraid. I just have to remember that Dad is not alone. God is with him. He will help him know how to answer the questions. God can keep Dad and our group safe if He wants to. And if He doesn't want to, well I guess God would have to have a really good reason not to keep Dad safe. Maybe Dad feels like he's in a lion's den right now. But Daniel's God is with him."

Jason nodded. "I will pray for you to trust God and not be afraid."

I encouraged Jason to leave. When that didn't work, I convinced him that it would look less like a Bible study if our Chinese friends didn't stay long.

As Jason's footsteps echoed down the stairway, Chuck phoned Susan to come over. I picked up my guitar and started playing chord progressions. G, E minor, C, D, G. I played it over and over then switched to A, D, E, A. I tried that several times until it became a tune. As I played the notes the words formed in my mind. "We will be true to thee till death." It was from the old tune "Faith of our Fathers."

John and Betty Stam. Communist soldiers pounded at their gate and escorted them away. John was allowed to write one letter. Then he and his wife were killed by Communist swords. His last written words were, "May God be glorified whether by life or by death."

I picked out the notes. "Faith of our fathers, living still in spite of dungeon, fire and sword."

Chuck's voice broke into my thoughts. "Interesting song choice."

"Yeah. Well, it's just one of the chord progressions you learn with the guitar. A, D, E, A. Pretty basic stuff."

"What are you thinking about, Daniel?"

"John and Betty Stam, I guess."

"They lived a long time ago, before even I was born. China has seen its share of martyrs, most of them Chinese. But we're in the twenty-first century now. Things have changed."

"OK. Maybe thinking about martyrs at a time like this is a little extreme. But what if we get kicked out of China? What would happen to our ministry? Who would teach our Chinese friends about the Bible? You said yourself you didn't come to China to see a few people saved and then leave them without teaching."

"I said that, and I still feel that way. But don't forget Susan and I have been working here several years, and this is the first trouble we've had. We've been able to do a lot. There's no reason to think that's all going to end just because they've taken your dad to their office to ask him some questions. You had that same thing happen to you, and you're OK. Right?"

I set my guitar down. "Yeah, but that was different. I made the stupid mistake of taking pictures of something that, I don't know, was a threat to security, I guess. They could tell I wasn't trying to do anything illegal. But they took Dad from a Bible study in his own home. He's spent seven months 'recruiting new believers.' They're not going to like that."

"Define recruiting new believers. Are we trying to get people to become Christians? Yes. Do we pass out tracts or preach in public? No. We simply answer people's questions when they come to us. The government keeps those phrases vague on purpose. They can mean what they want them to mean."

I decided that could be good or bad. "But Dad helped to start a house church. The house church meets in his house—well, apartment anyway."

"OK, but the PSB doesn't know that. Well, probably not anyway, though I imagine they know we have meetings here. They probably just want your Dad to pull back a bit and be more careful about what he says. If it becomes obvious he's up to something and they're not stopping it, they lose face."

Susan rang the doorbell. She had taken a taxi to our apartment to save time. Chuck explained the PSB's visit. He didn't leave out any details, but he made the whole story sound about like an outing in the park.

Then we each prayed for Dad; that he would answer wisely, that God would give peace to him—and us too. We prayed for the safety of our group and that our ministry wouldn't be hindered.

And then we played a game of Boggle, which doesn't sound very spiritual when Dad was facing the PSB, but it kept us from thinking about the worst things that could possibly happen.

At 10:15 footsteps echoed in the stairway, and Dad opened the door.

He stepped inside, closed the door and locked it. Then he grinned. "Well, they're not kicking us out of the country yet."

He collapsed onto the couch. Mom rushed to the water machine for a glass of water. He waved it away. "Thanks, but I've been drinking tea all evening. In fact, I spent most of the time waiting. The officials were extremely polite. They brought me tea and American magazines to read. Finally a Mr. Li called me into his office. He asked me three questions: Do you charge your English students? Have you ever baptized anyone? And what do you tell people about the government?"

Chuck ticked off the questions on his fingers. "Charging students. Baptizing people. Government." He sighed.

Dad smiled weakly. "The Lord was protecting us. I could answer all of those questions honestly with no problem."

"Which shows us that the precautions we are taking are exactly right. We've been very careful about these things."

"Yes. They could have asked me a lot harder questions, but they didn't." Dad ran his fingers through his thinning hair. "We have a lot to be thankful for."

"It was probably just a warning. We need to work harder to find a place to meet besides the homes of us foreigners." Chuck leaned forward. "But first we need to thank God for protecting you and our ministry."

Soon Chuck and Susan went home. Chuck's dental clinic opened at 8:30, and Dad had to teach the next day.

I went to bed, but I couldn't sleep. Had someone turned Dad in? We were moving our Bible studies back and forth between our home and the Harveys', but maybe that wasn't enough. Maybe the neighbor across the hall noticed that the same group of Chinese people showed up at our door a lot.

It could be the gate guard. When our visitors signed in, that gave him a written record of people in our house church. Our regular gate guard was pretty friendly, but the weekend guard had frowned at me last time I greeted him. Maybe he didn't like us. Or maybe the regular guard only pretended to like us to get information.

Maybe it didn't have anything to do with our house church. Maybe Dad had said too much about Christianity in his classroom. He tried to be careful, but when the textbook mentioned religion, he had said a few things about going to church and praying. At Christmas he was invited to give a lecture on American holidays. He had explained the basic facts of the birth of Christ for about five minutes.

I hoped I hadn't given something away. William knew far too much about our family for someone who had Communist parents and wanted to join the party soon.

Maybe I had said too much in Chinese class. I had actually given Liu Laoshi a book defending the Bible and creationism. But it was a legal book. That shouldn't cause any problem.

Chinese class reminded me of Adam. What about that scary conversation we had Monday morning walking to the gate? Adam had discovered my birthday was less than two weeks away. For some reason he and some of the other guys in class wanted to give me a birthday party.

Nice idea, but Adam had chosen the wrong person. I jiggled the coins in my pocket hunting for words. "Well, Adam, hey that's really nice of you, but I think my parents will plan something with our co-workers."

"Your co-workers? Who are they? Someone your dad works with?"

Oops. Chuck and Susan were only our co-workers in the missionary sense.

"I'm not really sure what they have planned, but they'll do something."

"So? We can do something too. You need a real party on your eighteenth birthday." Adam winked. "You're the only one in class who hasn't reached manhood yet."

"I think that I'm not really used to your kind of party. I mean, you guys usually drink at your parties, right?"

"Yeah. So what? At eighteen you ought to be old enough."

"Well, I don't drink alcohol, and I kind of stay away from parties that have alcohol."

"What's the big deal with alcohol? A party's no fun without alcohol."

"I don't need it to have fun. See, I figure I need all the brains I can get, and when you drink you don't think clearly. So why would I want to intentionally do something to make myself dumber?"

"Drinking helps you relax. If anyone needs to relax, you do."

"Well, drinking isn't good for my body, either, and a wimp like me doesn't need any more problems."

"I don't think science has actually made up their minds on the effect of alcohol on your health. Some doctors think alcohol is good for your health. Come on. One time can't hurt."

"Actually my parents don't want me to drink either. It's not just because I'm young. They don't drink either."

"So we won't tell your parents."

I sighed. "Look Adam. I know it's hard to believe, but I'd rather please my parents than please you. No offense."

Adam's eyes probed mine. I turned away.

"It's because you're a Christian, isn't it?"

"Yes."

"I thought so. Some people call themselves Christians, but they don't really do much about it. But with you it's important, isn't it?"

"Well, yeah. I guess so."

"You spend all this time with your Chinese friends. You're always talking about William and Jason. You even went to Jason's hometown for New Year's. I bet you talk a lot about being a Christian."

Silence.

"Did I tell you I saw Jason the other day? You introduced me to him one day, months ago, when I ran into the two of you at a noodle shop. Remember? Well, I ran into him last Tuesday at the same noodle shop. We ate lunch together. He's a really nice guy. I bet you talk to him about being a Christian."

Silence.

Adam slapped me on the back. "Come on, Daniel. You can tell me. What do you think I'm going to do, turn you in? Hey, I'm an American like you are. I believe in freedom of speech. If you want to convert the whole Chinese nation to Christianity, it won't bother me."

I had no answer, so I did what I always did when Adam mentioned dangerous things. I changed the subject. "Hey, I forgot to tell you. There's a new Mexican restaurant on Yi Huan Lou. I can't wait to go. Maybe our family will go there on my birthday."

I hadn't fooled Adam, but he didn't say any more about being a Christian. When we reached the gate, I was still talking about restaurants in the area.

Maybe Adam had gotten more out of me than I realized. Maybe Jason forgot to be careful and said too much to Adam. Maybe Adam found out about our house church and turned Dad in. But if he had turned Dad in, he wouldn't be talking about it, would he? Or would he purposely talk about it to make me think he wouldn't?

SEVENTEEN

Obsessed with the identity of Dad's informer, I slept little after Dad returned from his interrogation. Finally I squinted my eyes and read 6:30 on my alarm clock and gave up on sleeping. I missed Melody. With her I could talk stuff out. She would tell me when I made sense and when I was being an idiot. I would love to hear her tell me now that all this wasn't half as bad as I thought it was. I would love to think that I was being an idiot and had nothing to worry about. But this wasn't the sort of thing we dared talk about over the phone.

I tiptoed into our spare room to e-mail Melody on our family computer. I couldn't put much detail into an e-mail since it might be monitored, but Melody was used to reading my e-mails. She would know enough to pray for us.

Dear Melody,

I hope you're thinking of us. It is a difficult time. Some people are interested in Dad's work, but it's the wrong kind of people. He has had to answer some hard questions. We need to change some things and we're not sure how to do it.

I feel like I'm on a roller coaster. Think of me.

Daniel

All day long I worried about who had turned Dad in. I didn't feel like going anywhere, but Jason's class was cancelled. He called me on his cell phone and invited me to meet him at our noodle shop. I figured he wanted to find out what had happened to Dad. I had just talked to Adam on Monday about that same noodle shop. It seemed, somehow, like a bad omen. But I was a Christian. I didn't believe in omens.

I found the simple little shop and sat in the back with my back toward the wall. Tables filled. Though no one looked directly at me, I got a creepy feeling that someone was watching me. I shuddered. Of course, people were watching me. I was the only non-Chinese in the shop. People always watched me.

The cook stretched dough into long noodles and lowered them into boiling pots. Lunchtime traffic filled the sidewalks with people passing by close enough to feel the heat from the open air kitchen. Jason arrived, and we ordered.

The cook's wife pulled hot noodles from the pots and lowered them into bowls. She added a spoonful of vegetables to each and set them in front of us.

Jason stretched his arms out in front of him and folded his hands. His head bowed low into the prayer position I had taught him. "Father God in heaven," he prayed in strong fervent English, "Thank you for this food. We are so happy You give to us food every day. You give us very many good things. We are so happy You love us everyday."

My eyelids began to flutter, but Jason wasn't done. Once our family got settled in China, we realized that we could thank God for our food with confidence in restaurants. But we kept our prayers fairly short and tried not to flaunt them. Somehow, after

Dad's questioning the night before, I didn't think Jason needed to be quite this obvious.

"Thank You for my good friend Daniel who help me do very many things. I am very happy he come from America to be my friend. Help him to trust You and not be afraid. In Jesus' name, Amen."

I broke apart my disposable chopsticks. "You know, Jason," I whispered. "You don't have to fold your hands and bow your head when you pray. When we are in a public place like this I think a quick, quiet prayer is a very good thing."

"But you tell me I must pray when I eat meal. Christians must be thankful to God. Always I do this."

"Yes, that's good. But you know how those men came to our house last night and asked my Dad to go with them? Well, I think that means it wouldn't hurt to be a little more careful."

Jason frowned. "If we pray short prayers in restaurant, we are careful, not ashamed. Is it true?"

"I think so." I whispered a short report of my Dad's meeting with the PSB the night before.

"It is like the lion's den," he whispered back. "I think God help your father."

He was right. I didn't have the faith of Daniel in the Bible, but with all the suspicious people in my life, I felt like lions were stalking me. And that evening one of those lions showed up at my door.

I opened the door, not as wide as usual, and found William. He took that as an invitation and pushed in. His eyes sparked with excitement. "Brandon call me yesterday. He invite us to rock music concert Saturday evening. He think you will want to hear different kind of Chinese music. Do you want to go?"

An evening with William, guarding every word I said, listening to Chinese rock music. I couldn't think of anything I would enjoy less. How could I get out of this?

"I thought you didn't like Brandon."

William shrugged. "He is my friend. He asks me. I think I must go."

"Do you want to go or are you just going to make Brandon happy?"

"Brandon will be happy if I bring you."

"And if Brandon is happy maybe his mom will help you get a visa."

"Maybe she will do this. It is good. I may need a visa."

I frowned. "In American we call that *using people*. It's kind of like a bribe."

"I do not know this word."

"It's like, you know, maybe you wanted to get the government to do something for you, and they wouldn't do it. So you offer money to the right person, and then they will do it for you. That's a bribe."

William nodded. "I understand. It is good way to make things happen very quick."

I folded my arms. "But it's wrong."

"Why wrong? It help many things work."

How did I get into this conversation? More than that, how could I get out of it? "Forget it."

"Daniel, are you angry at me?"

"Never mind."

"But I do not understand what I say wrong."

"OK. A lot of people think you should be someone's friend because you like him, not to make him do something for you."

"It is American thinking?"

"Yes." I wanted to add, *And it ought to be Chinese thinking too.*

"We are friends. You teach me English. It will make me success . . . succeed. This is good way you help me."

"Yes. And you help me learn about China."

"What is different?"

I sighed. "Never mind, William. I don't think it is something I can explain."

"You are angry at me?"

"No. You're fine."

"You say about God, He wants very high quality. We are not good enough. Jesus is His Son. Jesus is good enough. If He is our friend, God thinks we are good enough. Is it true?"

"Yes."

"It is the same. We must have friends if we succeed."

How did God get mixed into a conversation about Chinese rock music? Was this a trap or what? William could have been the one to turn Dad in. Maybe without realizing it, I had said something dangerous about our family to William. He could have reported it. Didn't he say he would do anything to succeed? Well this was one trap I wasn't stepping into.

"Listen, William, if you want to go to the concert, go ahead. I don't really like rock music and I'm not going to pretend to like it to please Brandon."

Worry clouded his eyes. "Sorry, Daniel. I do not want to make you angry at me."

I tried to smile. "Don't worry about it. Maybe another time we can do something together."

I opened the door wider, and William took the hint.

At least I wasn't a hypocrite. At least I wasn't pretending to be Brandon's friend just to get something out of him. I wouldn't do that.

Or would I? I thought about all the things I had done with William during the last seven months. A lot of those things I didn't really want to do any more than I had wanted to go all those places with Jason during Chinese New Year's. But I wasn't trying to get William to do anything for me. OK, it didn't hurt my dad any to have me be friends with his boss's son. But it's not like he expected a promotion or anything. He just wanted to keep out of trouble so we could keep our ministry going. In fact this was a really stupid time to get cranky with his son. But other than that, we weren't looking for favors from the Wangs. We just wanted them to become Christians. It was different, wasn't it?

I didn't know what to think anymore. Suddenly all of my friends had become enemies. It was going to be pretty hard to witness to people if I viewed them with suspicion. But I had to. I didn't know who I could trust. I hardly trusted God these days. Maybe that was the problem.

I knew that God was in control. He wanted the best for us and our ministry. Dad had not been threatened, only politely questioned. Maybe it was a warning, but it wasn't the end of our ministry.

I thought about Philippians 4. Maybe I could trust God more if I filled my mind with positive things. I turned on my laptop and started a new file. *Save as?* I would call it my "Trust" file. It would help me trust God.

First I listed all the people that I suspected of turning Dad in. Beside their names I wrote nice things about each of them.

Then I made a list of my Christian friends in China. I read them over a few times, then deleted them. You can't be too careful about stuff like that.

Next I made a list of things I liked about China and fun things that I had done in China.

Lastly I typed out some Scripture verses that reminded me to trust God.

I finished that at 9:15. My last sleepless night had left me exhausted. I got ready for bed and drifted to sleep thinking of God's promises.

Sometime during the night I jerked awake. A cool breeze blew over me. Was that a sound?

I squinted my eyes to read the bedside clock. 3:47. My heart pounded wildly. I was too afraid to move.

A book slammed to the floor.

"Who's there?" I whispered.

A shadow crept across the floor, smashing into my guitar and vibrating the strings. It disappeared out the window.

I jumped out of bed and searched the darkness. The shadowy figure was sliding six floors down on a drainpipe.

I opened my mouth to yell, but my voice wouldn't cooperate. "Ssssttttstop!" I whispered.

But he didn't stop, and I wasn't going six floors down the pipe after him. Finally I forced my body into motion enough to switch on the light. My laptop was gone and my guitar would never play again.

I raced to my parents' room and beat on the door. "Thief!" I yelled. Then I flew down five flights of stairs in my pajamas.

Where was the gate guard? I sped to his cubicle and found him with his head on the desk—fast asleep!

EIGHTEEN

"That idiot stole my laptop. That's like stealing your soul!"

Mom turned my alarm clock to face her. 4:12. "No one can steal your soul, Daniel."

"OK. He didn't steal my soul, but he stole my thoughts, and that's almost the same thing. He's got my journal with practically everything I've thought about or done since we came to China. I'll never be able to replace that."

Mom plopped onto my desk chair. "I'm sorry. What about your school work?"

"It had about six months of school work too. I've got backups for some of that, but not the last month or so." I pounded my fist into a pillow. "Do you know how many months I slaved at Pizza Hut to buy that computer?"

Dad sat on my bed and rubbed the sleep from his eyes. His thinning hair stood straight up, and his pajama tops and bottoms didn't match. At that time in the morning he could have passed for a sixty-year-old. "Think, Daniel. Did you have any dangerous information on your computer?"

"Just last night I made a list of all our Chinese believers. But I deleted it right away, just to be safe. I'm sure glad I did. I've always tried to be careful not to put names on my computer or any information about our ministry. Anyone reading the information would know that I was a Christian, but I don't think it could harm anyone."

"Thank the Lord for that."

Mom frowned. "I wondered when we moved in if we should get window guards. The neighbors across the hall have them."

Dad fell back onto my pillow. "You'd think an apartment on the sixth floor would be safe. Somehow you don't expect anyone to climb five stories up a drainpipe."

Mom pulled a scratch pad from my desk and jotted something down. "Well, first thing this morning, after we get up for real, we need to call the landlord. We've got to ask him to put up window guards—even if we have to pay for them ourselves."

I picked up my broken guitar. "Maybe we should call the police. You never know. Maybe they could find the thief and get my laptop back."

Dad punched my pillow and snuggled into it. "Burglaries are so common here, I don't think the chances of that are very good."

"But shouldn't we try? Dad, you're falling asleep on us."

Dad jerked his eyes open and sat up. He watched me finger my splintered guitar and bent strings. "Look, Daniel, I care about this. But I didn't get much sleep last night after my little talk with the PSB, and this night isn't going any better. After one long evening of answering questions for the police, I'm in no hurry to call them back if it's not going to do any good. I'd rather they forget about us. So I doubt we'll be calling the police, but I'll talk to Chuck about it tomorrow." Dad glanced at the clock. 4:21. "Make that today—a few hours from now when decent people get up."

I never did get back to sleep after that.

How come everything seemed to be falling apart? Thursday night Dad got interrogated. Friday night a thief stole my laptop and smashed my guitar. Then Monday Dad got a note in his school mailbox asking him to come talk to Mr. Wang. Scrawled across the bottom were these words: "You may bring Daniel with you." What was that about? More trouble?

That afternoon Dad and I waited outside Mr. Wang's office for several minutes until he finished talking to someone else. Then he invited us in, seated us in comfortable chairs and offered us tea and cookies.

We were hardly hungry, but if he wanted to make this friendly, we wouldn't argue with him.

Mr. Wang sat behind his desk, leaned back with a forced casualness.

"Daniel, you have been a good friend to my son William. You have helped him so much with his English. He has enjoyed your friendship very much."

I sipped my tea. "Thank you Mr. Wang. I have enjoyed getting to know him too."

He studied my eyes. "William does not have many friends. Sometimes he can be . . . annoying. If he does something that you don't like, you can tell me. I do not want William to lose your friendship by an annoying little habit."

"Don't worry. William is fine. I'm glad to be his friend."

A smile flickered across his face. He turned to Dad.

"Now Brett. I received a visit from the Public Security Bureau. It seems you invite many Chinese people to your home. The PSB does not understand this."

Dad set his teacup on the coffee table, fiddled with it, set it in the exact center of a discolored water ring. "Is there a problem with that? Is it illegal to have Chinese friends in my home?"

"No. You may invite guests. But you must understand that China has laws that are important for foreigners to follow."

"I know that. I have tried to be careful about what I say in the classroom. When I gave my holiday lecture at Christmastime,

I did give a very brief account of the Christmas story from the Bible, but only for a few moments. I felt that was appropriate since I was talking about Christmas, which is a Christian holiday. Is that a problem?"

Mr. Wang leaned forward and rested his arms on the desk. His gaze bored into Dad, willing him to hear his words and grasp their full meaning. "I am supposed to tell you that you need to be more careful. Your work in the university has been quite good, but the PSB is concerned about other aspects. In China we have this ridiculous law. You need to be more careful about what you do that is not in keeping with China's religious policy."

Dad nodded slowly. "I understand. I don't want to cause any problems here. I hope you will tell me if I unintentionally do something that I shouldn't."

Mr. Wang smiled, but it didn't reach his eyes. "Of course. You are a good teacher. We don't want to lose you."

Dad and I nodded a polite goodbye and left. When we got home, we talked about what Mr. Wang said, and what he didn't say. He had never actually told us not to talk about religious things, only to be more careful about how we talked about them. It was a friendly warning, and we could only thank the Lord for that.

The next Saturday William invited me to the park to see the peach trees in full blossom. After talking to Mr. Wang, I could tell William still felt hurt about the last invitation I turned down. This time I knew I needed to go.

I rode the bus to the park and met William at the gate. The park was filled with Chinese who had come to see the delicate pink peach blossoms. Spring had prodded other plants into flowering too. A flower clock ticked beside a statue of a Chinese lion. Yellow mums formed the face of the clock and purple petunias replaced numerals.

Ducks quacked noisily at the pond, fighting for the bread which children tossed to them. Kites fluttered in the gentle breeze. Vendors sold kites and toys and every kind of snack food. Children threw rings to win stuffed animals. Adults danced to loud ballroom music which blared from portable sound systems. Intense mah jong games filled many of the nooks and crannies of the park.

William and I sat at a table by a water lily pond. He ate melon seeds. He had brought a pack of M&M's for me.

"Daniel, last time I see you, I think you are angry with me. I am sorry I make you angry. I know I say something wrong, but I do not understand what is wrong."

"No, William. You don't have to apologize. I am the one who should be sorry. When you came to my house, I was having a bad day. I had my own problems that were making me . . . worried, unhappy. So when I saw you, I was already unhappy, and I took it out on you. I'm sorry."

"It is OK now?"

"Yes. It is OK."

"Daniel, you are my good friend, but sometimes I do not understand your thinking. I want to succeed. I must succeed or bring shame to parents. I try my best to get good grades. I make friends that can help me. Always I worry. But you are different. Compared to me you are much smarter. But succeed for you is different. You do not want friends to help you. You do not find essays on internet. You study at home, but you take much time to go many places, see many things in Huajiang too. I think of course you want to succeed, but I do not understand. What do you want in life?"

"You're right, William. My definition of success is different from yours. I want to get a good education and get a good job when I'm an adult. But I'm not worried about making a lot of money, just enough money to live on. And I don't care about having a job that makes other people think I'm important."

"I must know. What do you care about?"

Jason's question flashed across my brain. *Careful . . . ashamed. What is different?*

I picked out ten red M&M's and popped them into my mouth. "Well, I know that they teach you in school that there is no God, that only weak people need God. But I believe there is a God. I mean, look at nature. Do you really think this world comes from a big explosion? Do you think all the animals and people started out as some little cell somewhere? Do you think we all evolved by chance?"

William's eyebrows knit together. "It is hard to understand."

"You're right. It's hard to understand and even harder to believe. I believe that God made the earth. He made it for people to live in. And He had people write a book to tell them how to live. That book is the Bible. God made me, and God loves me, and I want to please God. If I can do that, I don't worry about the other stuff."

"This is so important to you?"

"Yes. It is."

William formed a circle with his melon seed shells. "But for you it is easy. You please God, you please parents. For me it is different. I please God, I make parents angry."

"I know. I wish it were different. I guess I just feel that pleasing God is the most important thing in the world."

He swept all the shells into his hand and dumped them into a nearby trash can. "I wish I may become Christian like you. If Jesus become my friend, God think I am good enough. But my father say it is time to join Communist Party. He join Party at eighteen. He think I should do same. Next month I become nineteen."

We started strolling through the park. We stopped at the top of a rounded, Chinese-style bridge. I leaned on the concrete railing and waited until some people passed by. "I'm sorry, William. I know it is hard. I can't tell you what to do. But, well, if you want my advice, I'd say you should put off joining the Communist Party for as long as you can. Once you join, well, it's pretty hard to change a decision like that, isn't it?"

William nodded sadly. "I know this. I wish it is not true. I think be Christian is good, but for me be Christian is impossible. I must join Communist Party."

What more could I say? Peer pressure was hard enough. In this case parent pressure was worse. I couldn't really tell him to forget what his parents said and listen to me.

My outing with William left me quiet and grumpy. I used to think I might be accomplishing something in China. Living here wasn't easy, but when you saw people getting saved or growing it was worth the inconvenience. But lately I felt I was pouring out my life for nothing. William was supposed to be my one soul, my one person that I would lead to the Lord. His salvation would prove God could use me as a missionary. It would show me that all the hours I spent trying to be his friend were worth it. But being a Christian could only secure his eternal destiny. It wouldn't help him get a better job or make his parents proud. How could Christianity compete with the Communist Party?

After supper I wandered into my bedroom to write in my journal. I glared at the empty place on my desk. My laptop was gone and my journal with it.

I shuffled into our little office and started my parents' computer. I could never replace the details of my eight months in China, but at least I could make lists.

I made a new file and typed "Goal" on the first line. "Win one you-know-what during my time in China." After that idiot stole my laptop I wasn't going to forget to be careful.

Next I typed "Who????" William was out. Chuck was working on Peter. Mom and Dad were each doing Bible studies with unbelievers who we were praying for. But who could I win?

Failing to come up with an answer to that question I hit "enter" and typed, "Problems: Who to tell???? How much to say???? Careful . . . ashamed. What is difference?????????????????"

This was no good. I wasn't coming up with answers, only more questions. I saved my work, more from habit than the worthiness of my thoughts. I turned off the computer and tried to read a book.

What did I have to show for eight months of living in China? I had tried to help Jason. Instead I had taught him to show disrespect for the government and be ashamed to witness. He had learned to be confident in praying before meals, which was perfectly legal, until I corrected him.

OK. I had made some mistakes. At least I had played the guitar and taught our church their first Christian songs. I had even considered teaching Jason how to play some simple guitar chords and leaving him my guitar, but my guitar wouldn't be playing any more chords now.

But my time in China hadn't been a total waste. I had seen one part of China and learned a lot. I might not have much to show for my ministry, but I could tell stories and talk about China. I would buy some quirky souvenirs and talk to the kids in our Children's Church in Seattle about China. If fact, with only two months left I needed to begin shopping. Next time I saw Jason, I'd have to ask him where to find a good place to shop.

Jason offered to take me shopping the next Saturday. We met at my house and rode the bus across town to an outdoor market. Jason said the area was known for having some of the cheapest souvenirs in Huajiang.

Down a dark alley we found a stall where a lady sold scrolls with ornate Chinese calligraphy. For fifteen yuan she would write out any saying you wanted. I had seen a great Scripture lesson taken from the old Chinese character for "righteousness." Would it arouse suspicion if a foreigner ordered such a thing?

I was about to ask Jason about it when a classmate of his walked up. He was well-dressed, almost American looking.

"Li Jing, who is your friend?" he asked.

Jason smiled. "He is Daniel, my American friend. Daniel, I must introduce you to He Ming." He pronounced it *Huh Ming*. "He is my classmate with best English."

"I'm not a very good singer but at least I'm good at humming." He Ming grinned. Good English and a sense of humor too. "You can call me Mark."

We chatted for several minutes. Jason told Mark we were buying souvenirs for me to take back to America. "This market has very cheap souvenirs. Daniel can buy many souvenirs here."

Mark shook his head. "Daniel doesn't want cheap souvenirs. He wants quality souvenirs. How can he impress girls with cheap souvenirs? My uncle sells very nice chops." He turned to me. "You can get a chop with your Chinese name and use it to stamp your name on your letters. My uncle has chops with high quality jade and onyx handles. He will give you a good bargain. Come. I will take you there."

We hurried out to the main street where Mark called a taxi. After riding the bus forty-five minutes to get to this market, I wanted to see a few more of the stalls. But Jason didn't seem to mind. In minutes we were swerving from lane to lane, heading for a totally different section of town.

When we arrived at the chop store, Mark and Jason each shoved bills toward the taxi driver. The taxi driver grabbed Mark's. Somehow I could never be quite pushy enough to pay my own way.

Mark's uncle was reading a newspaper when we arrived. He set it aside and brought us cups of tea. He led us to the most expensive chops first and pointed out the patterns in the onyx and the quality of the jade. Then he showed us some cheap wooden ones which would stamp your name just as well. But they wouldn't look like much of a souvenir. From there he showed us some in a medium price range which were still "a fine choice."

Jason whispered, "Daniel, this is very good prices. I think we are lucky to meet He Ming today."

After about fifteen minutes I chose a chop handle and left an order for the uncle to make a chop with my Chinese name.

From there Mark led us to many other shops. He knew many of the owners personally. Some offered us tea. I was sure they were giving us lower prices because Mark was along.

I considered a heart necklace for Melody. Nah. It was nice and the price was right, but she might think I meant something romantic by it. I bought her a stuffed panda bear instead.

Jason kept thanking Mark for helping us find such good bargains. Hours later we found a bakery with a few tables and chairs in it to get off our feet. Mark picked out some pastries. Jason started down the street to find a place to answer nature's call.

I chose a pastry with a cream filling. "Mark, it's really nice of you to take us shopping. I found a lot of things to take back to America."

"It's OK. Any friend of Li Jing's is a friend of mine."

"Have you known Jason, uh, Li Jing very long?"

"Yes. Li Jing and I have been classmates for many years. He told me about his American friend. Finally I meet you. You spend a lot of time with Li Jing, don't you?"

"Yes. Li Jing is very kind. He has taken me lots of places and taught me about China. At Chinese New Year's he even took me to his home in the country."

"I know. Li Jing told me. He was very happy that you could see his home." His face turned serious. "Maybe it wasn't comfortable for you. In China the country is . . . well, it is like China long ago."

"I got along OK. I was really glad I could see the country. Since I came to China I've spent all the rest of my time in Huajiang."

"You help Li Jing with his English, don't you?"

I nodded. "Well, yes. And he helps me with my Chinese. I think he's learning faster than I am." I laughed.

"And you study the Bible together too."

I caught myself just beginning to nod and pretended to choke on my pastry. Mark asked the bakery owner for a drink.

"Thanks," I said. "I'm OK now."

"Yes. We were talking about Li Jing. You study the Bible with him, don't you?"

"We talk a lot about China and America and different customs and stuff like that."

"And the Bible, right? They say you really can't understand American culture if you don't know a little about the Bible."

I searched my pockets for a packet of tissue so I could wipe pastry crumbs off my face.

Mark grinned. "You can tell me, Daniel. I know Li Jing is a Christian. We're good friends. Some day I want to study the Bible too."

Careful . . . ashamed. What is difference?

"Well, we talk about the Bible sometimes. I mean, I'm a Christian too. Christians like to talk about the Bible to other Christians."

"Of course. I would like to study with you, but I live a long way from your apartment. Do you study together in your apartment?"

I nodded—slowly.

"Very good. I know Li Jing is really happy to study with you. How long have you two been studying the Bible? Five or six months?"

"A bit longer. My family has been in China eight months now."

"You said that. What do you like about China?"

I began exercising my gift of gab, the way I did with Adam. I listed every place I had visited and anything I could think of about China. Inwardly I was sighing with relief. Mark might be a good friend of Jason's, but the conversation still made me nervous. I didn't know why. Jason had probably already talked to him about being a Christian. Maybe Dad's visit to the PSB had made me paranoid.

Or so I thought. William called on Tuesday night and invited me to a tea house. Tuesday night was an unusual time for us to get together. Did he have something on his mind?

He sure did. As soon as our tea came William jumped right to the point.

"Is Jason angry with you?" he whispered.

"Why should he be angry at me?"

"You did not hear what happen in class?"

"No. What?"

"You tell He Ming that Jason study Bible with you. Is it true?"

I blinked. "How do you know that?"

"He Ming is class monitor for teacher who is very strong Communist Party member. Teacher always try to please Party, get high position. My father is Party member, but he is not like teacher. She does not care about people, only position. He Ming work for teacher. Always he listen. Always he ask questions. He tell information to teacher. Teacher give him extra privilege. Teacher tell Party. This make teacher and He Ming succeed in Party."

"But I thought He Ming was a good friend of Jason's. He took us around to a lot of good shops and helped us get good prices. He already knew Jason was a Christian."

William shrugged. "Everyone know Jason is Christian. One day at art class teacher talk about religious paintings in history. She ask who at class is Christian. Jason raise his hand. This is not secret. But study the Bible at foreigner's house, Jason never tell that."

"So what happened? Did Jason get in trouble?"

"Teacher make Jason come to front of class. She say, 'Li Jing, why you study Bible?' " William shook his finger at an imaginary Jason. " 'You are weak! Only weak people need God because they are not strong, need help. Science teach us there is no God. You are stupid not to know this! You listen to foreigners with their bad teaching against science!' So long time she shame Jason. Then she make whole class take very hard exam."

"Oh no! I feel really bad. And really stupid. He Ming acted like he already knew about our Bible studies and he asked me . . . what? I guess he asked me where we studied, how long we had been studying. I didn't say much but I did answer his questions."

William frowned. "Why do you do this, Daniel? He Ming do this because he want good things from Party, but you . . . why do you do this?"

NINETEEN

"I want to go home."

Mom stopped stir frying her vegetables. Dad dumped the chopsticks in a pile on the half-set table. "What do you mean?"

"Tomorrow's my birthday. I only want one thing. I want to go back to Seattle—soon."

I told them what happened with Jason and He Ming who I called Mark. "My one big prayer since I came to China was that I would never endanger a Chinese believer. Well, I flunked. I could say that Mark tricked me, but the truth is I know better. I should have played dumb or changed the subject. Now I've humiliated Jason."

Dad frowned. "I'm sorry, son. I can imagine how you feel, but we all make mistakes."

"Not that kind of mistake. You guys and Chuck and Susan, you would never get trapped into telling a total stranger incriminating evidence against our Chinese friends. I thought my job in

China was to disciple Jason. Well, I do a great job of that! I tell him to rebel against the government. I teach him to be ashamed of praying in public. He wants to witness, and I discourage him."

"You are teaching him to be careful. Jason needs to learn that. You've just been telling us how Jason got in trouble because you let your guard down one time and weren't careful enough."

"Yeah, well, when are you careful, and when are you ashamed? I don't even know anymore."

"That balance is something we all work at, Daniel. It isn't easy to get it right. But that doesn't mean we give up."

"It doesn't mean *you* give up, but me? I can give up. I mean, I was only going to stay for two more months anyway. I'm doing more harm than good with Jason. William's not going to believe. He has already decided to join the Party instead to help him succeed. I might as well go back to Seattle. I can live with Aunt Jenny and get my job back at Pizza Hut. I could work almost five months before Bible college. That ought to help my school bill."

"You have it all figured out, don't you."

"Yep."

"There's nothing wrong with earning money for Bible college, but I really hate to see you leave now, like this."

"Like what?"

"Quitting. Giving up because it's hard. Leaving early because you don't have what it takes to stick to it. You only have two months left. Why not wait until then to go back?"

"Because I want to go back now. I've nearly finished my home-school work. Why stay here when I can go back and earn money? So can I go or what?"

Mom and Dad just stared. I suppose they were thinking what a total failure their son turned out to be.

"Look, I've stuck it out for eight months. I've learned some Chinese. I've eaten all kinds of weird food. I've had my laptop and my bike stolen. What more do I have to do?"

Dad set two chopsticks by each bowl. "Nothing. If you want to go back now, you can. But I think you might regret it if you do."

"Well, I don't. I mean, in the beginning it was an adventure. New places, new food, new friends. But the novelty has worn off. I'm tired of always worrying about doing something wrong. Even when I'm with Chinese friends, I can't relax. I have no control over my life. And the worst part is . . ."

Mom shook the vegetables from the wok into a bowl.

Dad scooped rice from the rice cooker into our bowls. He turned to me. "What is the worst part?"

"Well, I thought these people were supposed to be hungry for the gospel. I thought we were supposed to see lots of people come to Christ."

"Several people in our group have gotten saved this year."

"Yeah, well, none of them needed *my* help to do it. I made a bargain with God. I told Him I was willing to come here for ten months, totally change everything about my life, face the danger, quit living mainly for myself. But I asked Him for one thing. I asked Him for one soul, for one person who I could personally lead to Christ during my year here. Well, William's the only un-saved person I know very well, and no way is he getting saved. So why should I waste two more months of my life here?"

"Those bargains with God don't always work out too well. Maybe it's because our bargains manipulate God to do our will. God doesn't manipulate too easily. You're usually better off try-ing to do His will instead of making Him do yours."

"Maybe so, but I just don't get China anymore. I don't even know what I'm trying to do here. I'm ready to go home . . . to Seattle."

Dad sat at the table. "Well, Daniel, if you're sure that's what you want, we'll ask Ken to start looking for tickets. You have put up with a lot here. I know it hasn't been easy. You've stuck it out for eight months. I wish you'd stay until June, but you can leave if you want."

"I have to leave," I whispered. "I hate this place. Look, can I eat later? I really don't feel too good."

I forced myself to walk slowly and calmly to my room. Inside I closed the door and leaned against it. "I hate this place," I whispered over and over again.

The Great Wall poster mocked me. "You cannot be a true hero until you have climbed on the Great Wall." I would never be a hero now. My parents had promised to take me to the Great Wall when I left China in June, but there was no time now.

The Proverbs 3:5 and 6 poster whispered its message to me.

"Sorry, God. You're just going to have to direct my path right back to America. I've got to get out of here."

Tears streamed down my cheeks, but I was careful to sob quietly so Mom and Dad couldn't hear me. I didn't want to hurt them any more than I had to.

The next evening Chuck and Susan came for supper. I blew out the candles on the cake with one unspoken wish. *I want to get out of here.*

Mom and Dad gave me a blue striped shirt and an IOU for a plane ticket with a departure date of April 15. Ken had reserved a seat for me. Dad just needed to get the money to him.

Chuck and Susan gave me a poster from the panda reserve for my dorm room. I had hoped to fly to Chengdu and see the pandas, but it was too late now. I kept sneaking peeks at my watch, waiting for Chuck and Susan to leave and my birthday to end.

Mom and Susan went to the kitchen to wash dishes. The phone rang and Dad answered it. From his position on the couch it looked like he'd be awhile. Chuck sat across the dining room table from me—bad news when I wanted him to accept my decision, not question it.

Chuck doodled a birthday cake on his napkin. "So. You're going back to the States early."

"Yep."

"You want to talk about it?"

"Nope."

"Why? Are you afraid I'll try to talk you out of it?"

"Yep."

"I see."

"What?"

"Well, you must not be very confident about your decision if you're afraid I'll talk you out of it."

I folded a napkin into an origami crane. "Look, I don't even know what I'm doing here. I don't begin to understand Chinese culture. So much seems unfair, wrong. Like bribes and being friends with people to see what you can get out of them. And obeying a government that is anti-God. And that whole group thing you told me about that means you never get to do what you want to do. It's so twisted, it just feels wrong, and I don't even know why anymore."

"Ah. Cultural issues. You're trying to figure out what's biblical and what's cultural. That's good."

"Good? I've been here eight months, and I'm doing more harm than good."

"Where did you get that idea?"

"You heard about what happened with Jason. When I came to China, I knew I was in way over my head. I knew I would be limited in what I could do without knowing Chinese and Chinese culture. I was OK with that as long as I didn't endanger a Chinese believer. I prayed over and over again just for that. And look what happened. Jason was targeted and shamed in front of his whole class."

"So that's what this is about."

I held up a lopsided crane. "Yeah."

"What happened to Jason isn't very nice, but that's not exactly danger, just humiliation."

"What? That's not bad enough?"

"It's not good, but Jason will live through it."

"But his classmates won't forget he's a Christian. They won't forget how they were punished because of what he did. In a country where relationships are everything, Jason will be feeling the effects of what I did for many years."

"You made a mistake, and Jason suffered for it. It's far easier to suffer for your own mistakes than have someone else suffer for them. But we all make mistakes. What if we all go home? Our friends would be safer, but if they don't get saved, they'll go to hell. Is that the kind of safety you want for them?"

"No."

Chuck scribbled a big question mark with little baby question marks all around it. "Half the time I don't know what I'm doing here either. We try to reach the people God brings to us. We give them the gospel, a little bit at a time. We see how they respond to one bit before giving them more. I remember when we found out that Kenneth was saved. A month earlier he had received Christ. No one guided him through the process, and he never bothered to tell anyone. Every now and then we find out Max has picked up a new spiritual truth from reading the Bible on his own. We've been feeling our way along like that for a couple of years now. And when we stop to count all the people who come to our house or yours for various Bible studies, we have more than twenty. Most of them are saved. We've started a church, and we hardly know how it happened."

"That's great. But you don't need me to keep the church going."

"We're building a church on the devil's doorstep, and I'm excited to be a part of that. It's rewarding to see results for your labor. But Daniel, there's a more important reason I stay in China." He drew a target. "I can go to sleep every night knowing I'm right in the center of God's will."

"Yeah, well, I figure I've done my time in China, and it's time for me to leave. If I leave now, I'll have five months to work before Bible college. That sounds like a pretty good idea to me."

"And that *pretty good idea*—is that the center of God's will?" He tapped a bull's eye on the target. "Are you sure that's His best for you?"

How could you answer a question like that? I didn't even try.

"So. You're going to live with your Aunt Jenny and work at Pizza Hut."

"Yeah. I'll get to see my youth group. I might even fly out to see Melody at college."

"You plan to drive when you get back?"

"Sure."

"You sure you want to do that? It's not always safe on the roads in Seattle."

Seattle . . . unsafe? "It's a heap safer than here in China."

"You could still have an accident."

"I'll risk it. I'll drive carefully and all that, but if something happens, I guess I'll deal with that when it happens."

"Sounds dangerous to me."

Weird. This still didn't make sense. "Why? Have you forgotten how safety conscious America is?"

"Any place can be dangerous, Daniel. You measure the risk of driving in Seattle. Then you drive carefully, but you drive. You measure the risk of witnessing in China. Then you witness carefully. Life is full of dangers but there's no place as dangerous as being out of God's will."

The clock ticked loudly, accentuating the silence. I didn't want to be rude but it was my birthday. I moved to the couch and studied my panda picture, willing the Harveys to leave.

But if it was hard to tell Chuck and Susan about my decision, it would be harder to tell Jason. Jason had his Saturday class cancelled and had gone home for the weekend. Monday I arranged to meet him at the Fountain of Life Coffee House near his dorm.

Fountain of Life was a quiet little coffee house on the second floor of a ten story building. The owners differed from us in doctrine but seemed to be sincere Christians.

I scanned the Christian books on a bookshelf. It was a mini-library available to their customers. I would remember this little Christian oasis when I returned to the States.

Jason arrived before long, and we ordered mango smoothies.

I sucked my straw quietly. This would be our last private conversation. "William told me about what happened at school with Mark and your teacher. I really feel bad about it. Mark told me he knew you were a Christian, and he asked if we studied the Bible together. You seemed so happy that he was giving us bargains that I decided you must be good friends."

"You are always careful. You even tell me I must be careful. So I did not think you will tell him about our Bible study."

"I know. It was the stupidest thing I have ever done. I'm really sorry."

"It is OK, Daniel. You are very good friend to me. Always you help me understand life of Christian."

"I know I've learned more from you than you've learned from me. But I need to tell you something. I have a chance to go back to America early and earn some money for college. I'm not going to stay in China as long as I thought."

"When will you go?"

"Friday."

"This week on Friday? Four days after today?"

I nodded.

The sparkle in his eyes died. "I think you long for America. Of course you want to see friends again."

"Sure. That will be good. And I'll be able to work for nearly five months. That will really help me pay for Bible college."

"It is good for you. For me it is very sad. Who will teach me Bible?"

"Chuck and Susan and my parents. And you can still come to all the Bible studies after I leave. I have something to give you too."

I pulled a brown paper bag out of my backpack and handed it to Jason.

He pulled the end open. "It is your Bible."

"Yes. It's a study Bible. The notes are just written by people. I mean they're not inspired like the Bible words. But they will help you understand the Bible. I can buy another study Bible in the States."

Jason ran his finger along the shiny gold pages. "Thank you, Daniel. I will use it all my life. I will improve my English so I may understand it better. But I will miss you. You are my only Christian friend of same age. We do very many things together. I see you, and I see how Jesus is like. Before, I think I have two more months to ask you many things I do not understand about Bible. But now . . . what do I do?"

"You'll be all right. Maybe Peter will get saved, and you can help each other. I will pray for you every day."

"I need you to pray for me. I will not forget our friendship. But I must tell you something. My Grandmother is very sick. Doctor in Zhushan say she will not live."

"Really? I had no idea. I'm sorry Jason."

He smiled. "But I can tell you good news. Big surprise. Grandmother tell me she become Christian."

"How? Did you lead her to the Lord? You know. Help her get saved?"

"At New Year's I leave Bible to her. I tell her read Matthew, Mark, Luke, John. She say missionaries tell about Jesus more than sixty years ago. Now she believe. She know she sins, Jesus died for her. Now when I go home to Zhushan there is two Christians."

"That's incredible Jason! I am so happy for you."

I wished I knew the names of the missionaries who had lived in Zhushan. Maybe they weren't alive today, but I would love to tell their children that a seed of the gospel they had planted in a heart more than fifty years ago had started to grow.

Fifty years from now, would anyone in China remember Daniel Wheeler had been here? Maybe Jason would remember me. Would he say, "He was very kind though his Chinese was poor?"

I see you, and I see how Jesus is like. No, Jason, don't judge Christ by what I am like. I don't need that kind of pressure. I'm just an ordinary guy. I don't have my act together. I have lots to learn, and right now I don't understand half of what I have learned.

I didn't want to think about leaving my friends in China, and I didn't have much time to think about them. Preparations to leave used every moment of my time. I had to cancel my Chinese class and explain to Liu Laoshi why I was leaving. I did laundry and hung it on the balcony, blowing a fan on them to dry them faster. I sorted and packed. Max, Sunny, and Daisy took our family out to eat Tuesday night. Kenneth, Jason, Cloudy, and Peter took me out Wednesday. Chuck and Susan invited us to their house my last night in China. I called William on the phone and told him goodbye. He wanted to take me somewhere too, but my time was gone and anyway, I hated goodbyes.

By Thursday afternoon I still had lots of packing to do. I pulled down my Great Wall poster, crumpled it into a tight ball and threw it into the trash.

I found the notebook that I had prepared for Jason. I had written the lyrics to Christian songs and guitar chords in it. But my guitar was ruined and it was too late to teach Jason anything. I tossed the notebook.

I opened the pocket notebook that I had brought to China. I had copied my first Chinese phrases into it from a Seattle library book. *Xie xie*. Ten months ago that was a new and awkward phrase. Now I could speak about as well as a five-year-old. Great accomplishment. I dropped the notebook into the trash with my Chinese text book. I wouldn't need them anymore. Maybe Brittany could talk to Liu Laoshi about creation.

Halfway through a novel an M&M wrapper marked my place. William was always buying me M&M's. Would I ever eat them again without thinking of him? I had hoped and prayed that William would be the one Chinese soul I led to the Lord. But William had chosen the Communist Party instead. Maybe I was wrong to bargain with God in the first place. The Bible never promised me one soul in ten months. I had asked God for one soul so that I would know he wanted me to be a missionary. But maybe that's not what He wanted. I could always be a math teacher like my dad.

I zipped open my carryon and pulled out my plane ticket for the next day. I hated this place. I had to get out of here, didn't I? What did it matter that I had learned to like a dozen kinds of Chinese pastries? In America I could eat donuts. I would never have to wrestle with my conscience over eating blood in America. My legs would probably go flabby when I quit climbing stairs all the time. I wouldn't miss karaoke or Chinese rock music. I wouldn't miss the traffic and the pollution.

I would miss my Christian friends though. I couldn't imagine sitting in our Seattle church with its musicians and offertories and well-behaved kids who skipped off to Children's Church. Our church had three pastors, six piano players, and an army of teachers. It had deacons, trustees, nursery workers, and club leaders. And a whole committee just for hospitality. It just seemed wrong that one church could have so many workers when China needed them so badly.

I pictured my friends from youth group. Would they ever get excited about learning something new in the Bible the way Jason and Max and Daisy did? I had changed in China. Would I fit in in Seattle anymore?

But, hey, I couldn't stay in China forever. I always knew I'd have to leave to go back to college. And it just made sense to leave early enough to make some college money. Right?

But if my decision was right, why did it feel so early? The decision was right, but the timing felt wrong. Why was there so much unfinished business?

I fingered the departure date on my ticket. April 15. In June I could leave China, like Chuck said, in the center of God's will. So what was April 15? Maybe it was the very edge of God's will, still on the target but as far from the bull's eye as possible. Was that far enough to be dangerous?

I flipped the pages of the ticket to the fine print and scanned the words. Non-refundable ticket. Well, maybe it wasn't God's will to leave quite yet, but now that I had bought the ticket, two more months couldn't be worth over a thousand dollars.

I grabbed a garbage bag and walked around the room collecting all the cheap stuff I'd bought in China, travel brochures for Beijing and mementos of silly adventures that no one in America would ever care about. I filled the bag and tied it shut. I raced down the stairs and set the bag by the dumpster before I could have second thoughts.

With the trash gone I stuffed everything else into my suitcase. Who cares how I packed my clothes? They'd get wrinkled anyway.

That evening Chuck and Susan tried to make supper a cheery goodbye. It didn't work well, and we didn't stay long. When we got home, I stuffed a few more things in my bags and stacked them by the door, ready for my departure in the morning.

Mom hugged me. I wasn't ready to start the goodbyes but tears streamed down her face. She rubbed them away with her thumb. "Sorry, Daniel. I always knew we'd have an empty nest someday. I was preparing myself for June, but I guess I'm just not ready for it yet. You will leave a real hole in our home."

I realized then that Mom was getting the tears done early. If I knew Mom, tomorrow at the airport she'd put on a brave face. She'd bite her lip and blink away the tears and make it easy for me to go. Grandma had done the same thing when we left Seattle.

Dad was getting teary-eyed on me too. He cleared his throat to steady his voice. "I had hoped you'd stay until June, but I don't want you leaving China defeated. You've done a lot of good here Daniel. You've grown up a lot this year. After you leave, I hope you can forget about these last weeks and remember all the brave things you did here and all the friendships you built."

In other words I had messed up big time, but they wanted me to feel good about my time here. Mom and Dad were protecting me because even though I was a quitter, I was still a kid.

If only I hadn't pushed Dad to buy that stupid airline ticket. I could stay and buy Jason a guitar and teach him how to play it.

I could invite Liu Laoshi home for supper and give her a good place to ask questions. William may have joined the Party, but Max was a Party member. Being a Christian and a Party member was complicated, but even joining the Communist Party wasn't the unpardonable sin. It wasn't quite hopeless.

In June I could have stood on the Great Wall and thanked God that I had done my best and finished my task in China. I could have left the results with God. Now I would always wonder how God would have used me if I hadn't left early.

But it was too late. I had made a mistake, a big mistake, an expensive mistake.

After a mostly sleepless night I jumped out of bed and showered quickly. Chuck and Susan couldn't come to the airport. Chuck had dental appointments and Susan had a Bible study. I had asked Dad to call Jason and William and tell them not to come to the airport. It would only make it harder to leave. I wanted a simple goodbye.

We checked in my luggage and found my departure gate. One more hour to kill before boarding. Mom and Dad gave me messages for relatives. I snapped a picture of a section of seats. The Chinese equivalent of handicapped seating, they were marked in Chinese and English "The old, weak, and pregnant."

Then Jason and William came racing down the corridor. They arrived at my gate, panting and sweaty, with grins on their faces.

I managed a smile. "Hey, I thought Dad told you that you didn't need to come to see me off. Don't you guys have school today?"

William handed me five packages of M&M's to eat on the plane. "Of course we must come to airport to say goodbye. You are our friend."

Jason gave me a book about the Great Wall. "Someday you must return to China. We will become heroes together."

I thanked them for their gifts. "Jason, I want you to have my bicycle. I know it doesn't look fancy, but it is a good bike. No one will steal it."

"Maybe your parents may ride bike."

"They don't need it. I would really like you to have it. I know you take the bus and train a lot, but it might come in handy."

"You are good friend to think of me, Daniel, but I wish I do not have bike, but instead you stay in China."

William's smile faded. "Jason and I worry. Jason tell me I should not tell you about He Ming and teacher and exam class must take. He say this make you feel very bad. Maybe it make you want to leave China. I tell Jason I also make you angry. I think we make you leave China early."

I shook my head. "Hey guys, it's not your fault. It has nothing to do with that." Was that last part a lie?

"Then why you leave China now?"

"I want to go back to the States and earn some money for college."

"Is it true? Is this only reason you leave now?"

"Well, I guess I have several reasons for leaving this early."

"Daniel, I must know." William's eyes begged me for an answer. "You say pleasing God is most important thing. Does God ask you to leave China now?"

I stared at the ground, zipped my carryon open and shut several times. "No, William. I'm leaving now for my own reasons. God wanted me to stay until June, but I didn't want to obey God. And you're right. When I told Mark about Jason and got Jason in trouble, I felt so bad about that, that it was part of what made me want to leave China. But it's not you guys' fault that I'm leaving. Actually, right now I wish I were staying, but I have a nonrefundable ticket. I would lose over a thousand US dollars if I stayed now."

William nodded. "I understand, Daniel. I wish to become Christian, but I must choose—Christian or Communism. Be Christian is very hard. If I do not join Party, I make my father unhappy. Maybe I will not succeed. You want to stay in China, but if you stay you lose much money. It is same thing. Sometimes person want to do something very much, but it is too hard."

I stared at William. My mouth probably hung open. My leaving China now was giving William an excuse not to become a Christian. I had made a huge mistake. I could fix it, but it wouldn't be cheap.

I grabbed Jason's sleeve. "Jason, you've got to help me get my luggage back."

"I do not understand."

"Come with me to the check-in counter. You must explain to the airline workers that I'm not going to America now. I must get my luggage off the plane."

"But you will lose very much money."

"That's right. I will probably have to start college a semester late so that I can work off the money I've thrown away on this ticket. But going back to the States now is a mistake, and I've got to make it right."

I hardly dared look at my parents. What would they think of me for wasting so much money?

Tears spilled onto their cheeks, but Mom and Dad wore matching smiles.

I grinned. "We'll be right back. It may take a while to round up my luggage. Then I want to go home."

On June 21 three "heroes" stood on top of the highest gate tower on the Juyong Pass section of the Great Wall. I was panting from the steep climb, and my legs shook like Jello. A year earlier I might not have made it to the top, but for ten months I had climbed five flights of stairs every day. I had reached my physical peak. My companions also rubbed their legs and mopped the sweat from their brows.

We gazed out the tower window at the long wall, a giant wriggling dragon, hugging the contours of the steep mountains. One window framed the "Piled Greens at Juyong Pass," a fitting description of the lush green waves of vegetation-covered hills. Another window showed a marble platform built more than seven hundred years before. Along the snaking wall below I could just make out Mom and Dad in pink and green T-shirts. They were huffing and puffing their way up the mountain.

William snapped pictures in every direction. "We must celebrate. Three friends climb Great Wall at same time, become heroes together."

Jason grinned. "You are right. I feel very honored your father buy me ticket to Beijing that I may come with you. It is very good way to tell Daniel goodbye."

William waved away his thanks. "It is nothing. I think when Daniel come with his parents to Great Wall, we must come too. So we must celebrate. I think each friend must tell a secret."

I wouldn't have to think twice about this secret, just how to word it. "I will go first. I know I'm going to miss China a lot, and I hope I can come back someday. My secret is: I am asking God to bring me back to China someday to live here for many years."

I didn't say the M-word. William knew a lot about me now. Jason had even brought him to our house church a couple times. In early May I had mentioned sin and Jesus dying on the cross. This completed the plan of salvation I had shared with him over several months. But William had turned down my invitation to believe. The last thing I did in Huajiang was tell God that I wouldn't bargain with Him anymore. If He wanted me to, I would be a missionary no matter what.

Two German tourists joined us in the tower. Jason handed them my camera and asked them to take a picture of the three of us. We started down the wall while the Germans caught their breath and rested their wobbly legs.

Jason stopped well out of hearing range of the Germans. "My secret wish is: William become Christian. Daniel come back to China. Three heroes be best friends."

William shook his head. His eyes clouded with sadness. "I know you want me to become Christian, but it is too late."

This was not the farewell I wanted. "It's never too late, William, unless you're dead."

William frowned, almost pouted. "No, for me it is too late. I cannot become Christian because . . ." He grinned. "I *am* Christian. That is my secret. I think my secret is best."

I stared at him. "How? When? I don't understand."

"My father say join Communist Party is good, but you say maybe it is not good. You say be Christian is better. So I tell father, please, I do not want to join Party now. I think about what you say to do to be Christian. I do this a few weeks ago."

"But you never said anything about it."

"I wait so that it will surprise you on Great Wall."

"Did someone talk to you about becoming a Christian and tell you what to do?"

"You did, Daniel. I know I must listen to your words. You say this is most important thing to you. You tell me I must be sorry for sin, believe Jesus died instead of me, ask Him to forgive me. Is it enough?"

Did William really understand what it meant to become a Christian? I thought about all the things that I had said to him, a little at a time, over the last several months. I had wanted to sit down with him and explain salvation all at once, one step at a time. I had wanted to pray with him and hear him pray and make sure he understood. I had wanted to record the date in my Bible and tell William that that was his spiritual birthday. This seemed so anticlimactic. But it was simple to William. Why should I complicate things?

I smiled. "Yes, William. It is enough."

I gazed past the layers of green mountains toward this vast land of over a billion people. So many needed to hear about Christ. Maybe someday I could tell a few more about him. Until then I would have to live in boring America. Tomorrow I would say goodbye to my two Chinese friends, brothers in Christ. It would be sad, but I could do it this time. It was time to leave. I had found the center of God's will, and I didn't want to live anywhere else.